GOOD GIRL

WICKED #1

PIPER LAWSON

I wanted to fall for a boy. Not a man. Not a *legend*...

The month I wrote my first piece of code, Jax Jamieson launched his third platinum album. The week I drank my first beer, he spent in jail. The day I got under his skin, I wound up on his tour.
And the night he gave me his hoodie... I fell in love forever.

I'm a good girl. And he's the vice I'd give it all up for.

1

HALEY

Nothing in twenty years prepares me for that man on his knees.

Naked to the waist.

Sweat gleaming on his shoulders.

The spotlight caresses the ridges of a body cut from stone as though it wants to follow him around forever.

Maybe it does.

But he's not stone. His skin would be warm, not cold.

Silhouetted hands reach for him over the edge of the stage, like something out of Dante's *Inferno*. Souls in hell grasping for their last chance at heaven. That seems misguided because the way Jax Jamieson grips a mic is straight-up sinful.

Next to the poster is a photo of four men in tuxes, gold statues in their hands.

We're attracted to gold for its sheen, its promise of something elite and revered and sacred.

My gaze drags back to the man in the poster. *Elite. Revered. Sacred.*

"I've read your resume. Now tell me why you're really qualified."

The dress pants that were a bad damn idea slip on the seat. The polyester scrapes along my skin, and I force eye contact with the woman interviewing me. "I reset at least two hundred undergrad passwords a week. And I make a lot of coffee. My roommate says I'm better than the baristas at her café."

"Excuse me?"

The printed job description sticks to my fingers. "'Technical support and other duties as appropriate.' That's what you mean, right? Rebooting computers and making coffee?"

She holds up a hand. "Miss Telfer, Wicked Records is the only private label that has survived everything from Napster to streaming. There are two hundred applications for this internship. Our interns write and produce music. Run festivals."

The woman looks as if she missed getting

tickets to the Stones' Voodoo Lounge tour and has been holding a grudge ever since.

Or maybe she was the next one into the record store behind me the day I found *Dark Side of the Moon* on vinyl in Topeka.

It's probably not a fair assessment. Under that harsh exterior, she could be genuinely kind and passionate about music.

Maybe I'm in *The Devil Wears Prada* and this woman's my Stanley Tucci.

"I run an open mic night on campus," I try. "And I'm a developer. I write code practically every day, and lot of people fork my repos on GitHub, and..." My gaze sneaks back to the poster.

"Don't get too excited," she warns. "Whoever gets this job"—her tone says it's not me—"won't work with the talent. Especially that talent."

Her final questions are nails in my coffin. Closed-ended things like if the address on my forms is right and if the transcripts I submitted are up to date.

She holds out a hand at the end, and I hold my breath.

Her skin's cold, like her heart decided not to pump blood that far.

I drop her hand as fast as I can. Then I shoulder my backpack and slink out the door.

The idea that the biggest rock star of the last ten years just saw me bomb—even if it was only his poster—is depressing.

I'm on the second bus back across Philly to campus before the full weight of disappointment hits me.

Are college juniors supposed to have run music festivals in order to pour coffee? Because I missed that memo.

I drop my backpack at our two-bedroom apartment, change out of my weird interview pants and into torn skinny jeans and my mom's brown leather jacket, then make two coffees and walk to campus, the UPenn and Hello Kitty travel mugs in tow.

"Excuse me." A girl stops me on the way into the café, right beside the sign that says *Live Music!* "There's a cover tonight."

"I'm here every week." My smile fades when I realize she really has no clue who I am. I point to my chest. "Haley. I get the bands."

"Really?" She cocks her head. "I've never noticed you."

The table at the back is de facto mine, and I set the travel mugs down before crossing to the stage.

The guy there frowns as he plays notes on his guitar with one hand, holding the headphones attached to the soundboard. When he notices me, a grin splits his face. "Haley. You like the new board?"

"I like it if it works." I take the headphones and nod at his guitar.

The first chord he plays is like the snapping of a hypnotist's fingers. My world reduces to the vibrations and waves from Dale's guitar.

I adjust the levels on the board. "There. You should be good."

Before I can lift my head, Dale's tugging the headphones off my ears. I jerk back like I've been scalded, but he doesn't notice my jumpiness.

His earnest brown eyes are level with mine. "Perfect, Haley. Thanks, Haley." *Did he say my name twice?* "You should sing with us tonight."

I glance toward the back of the café that's starting to fill. "Ah, I don't think so. I have to..." I make a motion with my fingers, and Dale raises a brow.

"Masturbate?"

I frown. "No. Code."

"Right."

I retreat to my table. The second chair is occupied.

"He tried to touch me," I say under my breath.

My roommate Serena tosses her honey-blond hair in a move that's deceptively casual. "That asshole." I roll my eyes. "You know some people communicate affection through touch. It's even welcomed."

"In hell," I say darkly as I drop into my chair. "We have our own bodies for a reason. I don't understand how some people think it's okay to stand super close to someone. And don't get me started on whispering." I shiver, remembering the contact. "If I wanted some random person to breathe on my face or grope me? I'd ask for it. I'd stand there waving a sign saying, 'Please God, run your unfamiliar hands all over my skin'."

"If you did that on campus, there would be a pileup." She winks before turning back to the stage, where Dale's bandmates have joined him and are getting ready to start their set. "Do you think Dale knows you have a man in your life? Because he's not getting so much as a 'maybe, if I'm drunk' unless his name is Carter."

"*Professor* Carter," I remind her. "He's twenty-eight and has a PhD from MIT."

"Whatever. He's cute in glasses. But he lost my respect when he bailed on your research assistant gig."

"He didn't bail. His funding fell through. It would've been perfect since I'd have more time to work on my program, but at least he's still supervising my senior project next year."

"That's his job." She snorts. "But I think he likes you tripping over him."

The look she shoots me has me shaking my head as I glance toward the stage.

Dale's no Jax Jamieson, but his latest is pretty good. The band's super acoustic, and they have a modern sound that plays well with a college crowd.

"Come on," Serena presses. "He doesn't love having college girls undressing him with their teenage eyes in Comp Sci 101? Yeah right. The man might be young enough to have danced to Britney Spears at prom, but thanks to Mr. 'Oops, I Did it Again,' you have two days to find a job so you don't get kicked out of the co-op program."

I flip open the lid of my computer. "It's my fault, not his. I suck at interviews. I haven't had to get a job before." Serena's smile slides, and I wince. "Okay, stop giving me the 'sorry your mom's dead' look."

"It's not just 'sorry your mom's dead.' There's a side of 'I can't believe you have to pay your own college.'" Serena's parents are loaded and generous.

"If it wasn't for the requirement to be employed by an actual company, I could spend the summer working on my program and enter it in that competition."

When my mom died last year, I took a semester off, lost my scholarships, and missed the financial aid deadline. Now I have to come up with tuition myself. I know I can figure it out because a lot of people do it, but if I win the coding competition in July, that'll help big time.

"Where were you interviewing today?"

I blow out a breath. "Wicked."

She shifts forward, her eyes brightening. "Shit. Did you see him?"

I don't have to ask who she means. A low-grade hum buzzes through me that has nothing to do with the music in the background.

"Jax Jamieson doesn't hang around the studio like a potted fern," I point out. "He's on tour."

"I don't care what kind of nerd god Carter is. Jax Jamieson is way better with his hands, and his mouth. Any girl would love having that mouth whisper dirty secrets in her ear. Even you."

I shift back in my seat, propping my Converse sneakers on the opposite chair across and fingering the edge of my jacket.

"I don't need to get laid. I've been there." I take a sip of coffee, and my brain lights up even before I swallow. "The travel agent promised Hawaii. Instead it was Siberia."

"Cold, numbing, and character building?"

"Exactly."

Sex is awkward at best.

What I can deduce from my own meager experience, porn, and Serena's war stories is that guys like to be teased, squeezed, popped until they burst all over you, at which point they're basically deflated hot air balloons taking up the entire bed.

And don't you tell them what you're really fantasizing about is when it will be over and you can take a scalding-hot bath.

"My vibe has more empathy in its first two settings than the guys on campus," I go on, and Serena cackles. "In fact," I say, lifting my UPenn travel mug, "I may *never* have sex again."

"Noooo!"

Her protest has me laughing. "Plato said there are two things you should never be angry at: what you can help and what you can't."

"Yeah, well. White men who got to wear bed sheets to dinner said a lot of crazy shit." Serena's green eyes slice through me. "Besides. I'm not angry. I'm planning." I raise a brow. "To find you a guy with a tongue that'll turn you inside out."

I shudder. "That's sweet. Truly. But I didn't come to school to get laid, Serena." Her fake shocked face has me rolling my eyes. "I want to do something that matters."

When I started college, my mom told me I was lucky to have been born now, and her daughter, because I'm free to be whatever I want. By that, she meant a famous painter or a rocket scientist, or straight or gay, an advocate for children or the environment.

It's not enough.

Serena's right. I'm obsessed with Jax Jamieson, but it's not because of his hard body or the way he moves or even his voice.

It's because Jax Jamieson *matters*.

He matters by opening his mouth, by lifting his guitar, by drawing breath. He matters by taking people's hopes, their fears, and spinning poetry with them.

Every time I sit down and listen to *Abandon* on vinyl on the floor of my bedroom, a coffee in my hands and my eyes falling closed, it's like he matters a little bit more.

If I ever meet Jax Jamieson, I'm going to ask him how he does it.

Before Serena can answer, my phone rings.

"Hello?"

"This is Wendy from Wicked Records. You got the internship."

Disbelief echoes through me. I glance over my shoulder in case I'm on camera for some reality show. "But what about the other two hundred applicants?"

"Apparently their coffee making left something to be desired. Be here tomorrow at seven thirty."

HALEY

I can't deal with the slippery pants two days in a row, so I borrow Serena's skirt that hobbles me at the knees.

On top of my sleeveless blouse, I stick my leather jacket.

For safety and comfort.

My backpack holds my computer and the completed paperwork HR sent me by email.

Walking through the glass doors should be easier than yesterday—hell, I got the job. But it's not, because I don't know what they expect. I want to ask, "Why did you hire me?" but the security guy checking my paperwork and processing my pass probably isn't the right person to answer.

"You're on two. Up the elevator."

The first two elevators are packed full, so I find a stairwell at the end of the hall.

When I open the door to the second level, I'm in another world.

Pristine carpet, white as snow. Paneled walls in a rich red color that should look retro but doesn't.

I peel off my leather jacket because it's warm up here and glance down the hall.

Wendy's office is supposed to be to the left. But cursing from the first door in the other direction pulls me in.

Inside, a guy who can't be much older than me surveys a computer rig I'd give my leg for. An error message lights up the screen in front of him, blinking like some doomsday prophecy.

"Can I help?" I ask. With a quick head-to-toe that ends on the pass clipped to my waist, he ushers me in.

"What the hell took so long?" the tech asks. "I called IT ten minutes ago."

It's moot to point out that I wasn't with IT ten minutes ago.

My eyes adjust to the low light as the door slips closed behind me. There are no outside windows, just the glass half panel facing the studio and a closed door that connects the two.

Someone's recording in here. The figure in the other room is facing away from the glass, bent over a guitar like he's tuning it.

I push aside the bubble of nerves. My focus is on the computer.

"Is ten minutes a long time?" I ask as I set my paperwork and my jacket on the desk. My fingers start to fly over the keyboard.

"It is when *he's* here."

I hit Enter, and the error message goes away.

It isn't until I straighten that his words start to sink in.

"When who's here?"

That's when I'm viciously assaulted.

At least it feels that way because two horrible things happen in such close succession I can barely tease them apart.

Hands clamp down on my bare arms from behind.

Hot breath fans my ear, and a voice rasps, "What the fuck is going on?"

Every hair on my body stands up, my skin puckering, and I do what any reasonable woman grabbed by a stranger in a vice grip would do.

I scream.

It's not a cry for help.

It's a bellow of rage and defiance. Like a banshee or Daenerys's dragons en route to scorch some slave traders.

Channeling strength I didn't know I had, I whirl on my heel and collide with a wall. My hands flail in front of me, lashing out at my attacker.

I'm not a puncher, I'm a shover. But when I shove, all that happens is my hands flex on a hard, muscled chest.

I trip backward, my grown-up skirt hobbling me as I fall.

I grab for the desk but only get my papers, which rain down like confetti as I land on my ass.

My heart's racing at an unhealthy speed even before I take in the white sneakers inches from my face.

"Jax. I'm really sorry," the guy behind me says. "I called Jerry ages ago."

Sneakers, as white as the carpet, are pointed straight at me. Dark-blue jeans clinging to long legs, narrow hips. A faded olive-green T-shirt stretches across his chest, like it started out too tight but gave out over dozens of wears. Muscular arms—one covered in a sleeve of tattoos—look like they lift more than guitars.

I force my gaze up even though I want to melt into the floor.

A hard jaw gives way to hair the color of dirt faded in the summer sun. It's sticking straight up in most places but falling at the front to graze his forehead. His nose is straight, his lips full and pursed.

His eyes are molten amber.

Dear *God*, he's beautiful.

I've seen hundreds of pictures of Jax Jamieson, watched hours of video, and even been to one of his concerts. But the complete effect of all of him, inches from my face, might be too much for one person to handle.

And that's before he speaks.

"I repeat. What. The *fuck*. Is going on?"

His voice is raw silk. Not overly smooth, like the Moviefone guy. A little rough. A precious gemstone cut from rock, preserved in its natural glory.

There are things I'm supposed to say if I ever meet Jax Jamieson.

I wrote them down somewhere.

"I'm Haley Telfer," I manage finally. My throat works as I shove a hand under me, shifting onto my knees to pick up the papers. "But you know that."

His irritation blurs with confusion. "Why would I know that?"

"You're standing on my Social Security number."

One of the papers is under the toe of his sneaker. I grab the edge of it, and his gaze narrows. What is it with me and pissing off these people?

Not that pissing off Wendy comes close to pissing off Jax Jamieson.

(Whom apparently I'm going to refer to with both names until the end of time.)

"Haley Telfer?"

"Yes?" I whisper because, holy shit, Jax Jamieson refers to people with two names too.

"You have ten seconds to get out of my studio."

———

The tech and I stand next to each other, peering through the glass studio door into the hall. My jacket's back on, not that the guy's coming anywhere near me because he thinks I'm a lunatic.

On the other side of the door, Jax exchanges angry words with a man in a suit.

"That's Shannon Cross," I say.

The tech nods, stiff. "Correct. The CEO showing up means one or both of us is fired."

"Well... which is it?"

We watch as Jax stabs a finger toward me and stalks off.

"I'm guessing you," my companion murmurs.

The door opens, and Shannon Cross looks at me. "My office. Five minutes." He turns and leaves.

After gathering my papers, I take the tech's directions to the elevator to the third floor. A watchful assistant greets me and asks me to take a seat in one of the wingback chairs.

Great. I've been here less than an hour, and I'm about to be fired.

Instead of spinning out, I study the picture on the wall and the caption beside it.

Wicked Records's headquarters. Founded in 1995, relocated to this new building in 2003. Employs two thousand people.

"Miss Telfer."

I turn to see Cross watching me from his door-way. He exudes strength, but in a different way than Jax. He's older, for one. Tall and lean, with hair so dark it's nearly black. The ends curl over his collar, but I can't imagine it's because he forgot to get a haircut.

His suit is crisply cut to follow the lines of his body. He was one of the men with all the gold statues in the picture yesterday. Yet on this floor, there are no pictures of him.

Weird.

He's made millions—probably billions—in the music industry. Formed stars whose careers took off, flamed out. In the golden age of record executives, he's one of the biggest.

I follow him into his black-and-white office, a continuation of the pristine carpet outside. It should look like something from an old movie, but it doesn't. It's modern.

A fluffy gray rug on the floor under a conversation set looks as if it used to walk.

I'm struck by the urge to run my fingers through it.

The photos gracing the walls here are black-and-white, but they're not of musicians or awards receptions.

They're fields and greenspace.

Err, gray space.

"Is that Ireland?" I blurt. "It looks beautiful."

I turn to find his gaze on me. "It is. My father moved here when I was a child."

I wait to see if he'll offer me a seat, but he doesn't. Nor does he take one as he rounds the black wood desk, resting his fingertips on the blotter.

"Miss Telfer, I understand you interfered with a studio recording session. And assaulted one of our biggest artists."

My jaw drops. "I definitely did not assault him. He started it."

I realize how childish it sounds. The memory of it has my skin shivering again, and I rub my hands over my arms. "Technically, he startled me. I was trying to defend myself. Every modern woman should have a knowledge of self-defense, don't you think?"

He doesn't nod, but he hasn't kicked me out yet, so I keep going.

"I know I shouldn't have walked in, but your tech had this 'FML' look I know from a mile away. I know the software. I use it in the campus music lab all the time. There's a compatibility issue with the most recent update, and..." I trail off as he holds up a hand. "I wanted to fix it."

Appraising eyes study me. "And did you?"

I realize Cross isn't asking me about my outburst but what I'd done before that. "Yes. Yes, I think so."

Cross' lips twitch at the corner. "Jax Jamieson is heading out on the final leg of his U.S. tour, and we're short on technical support. We could use someone with your problem-solving skills to back up our sound engineer."

"You're asking me if I want to go on a rock tour?" Disbelief reverberates through me.

"Of course not." His smile thins. "I'm reassigning you to a rock tour."

"He wants you to what?" Serena shrieks over the phone.

"Go on tour. Four weeks." From the way I'm hyperventilating in the bathroom stall, I'm surprised the force of it doesn't lift me clean off the linoleum. "Then I can choose to return to the studio and spend the rest of the summer making coffee. Or they'll sign a letter saying my co-op term was completed because I'm working around the clock."

"You have to do it."

"First, I have no idea what it means to back up a sound engineer on tour. And second, spending twenty-four hours a day with other people sounds like a special kind of hell." I yank a sheet of toilet paper from the roll and start the productive task of tearing it into tiny pieces. "I bet they all travel on a bus."

"The horror."

"It is!" I insist. "They probably sleep in a pile, and..." I hiccup, yanking at my waistband. "Dammit, this skirt is *really* tight."

My fingers find the zipper, yanking it down enough that I can breathe while Serena laughs. "When does it leave?"

"This afternoon. I'm supposed to report to this address and see the tour manager." I take a breath.

"You have to admit it's kind of poetic," she observes. "Plus, you're out of options. The point of the co-operative education program is to put your training into practice. If you don't have a job in the summer where you can practice, you'll get kicked out."

Which is the only reason I'm still here instead of halfway down the street.

"I've never had a real job before. I live behind a computer." I slap my forehead. "And I was planning on a job where I'd have time to work on my program with Professor Carter."

"Forget Carter. This is a sign. You're going to fuck Jax Jamieson."

This is the risk of being friends with Serena. She regularly makes statements that, although they may be entirely false, have the immediate effect of taking years off your life.

"Serena, it's not a sign. It's a mistake chased by a coincidence wrapped in a bad idea. Jax Jamieson isn't someone you fuck. He's someone you study and watch and learn from. He's someone you worship."

"Yeah, with your tongue." Shivers run through me. "You go to college to learn and study. A guy like Jax Jamieson is *exactly* who you fuck. He probably has to lift an eyebrow and panties drop. He could blow on a girl, and she'd come. Hell, if he so much as brushes past you in the hallway? I bet you could live off the contact high for the rest of your life."

"I interrupted his recording session."

A loud bang has me holding the phone away from my ear. "Sorry, I dropped you. What the hell, Haley? You met a rock star and got invited on his tour. This is amazing. So... is he?"

"Is he what?" I whisper.

"So hot you'll picture him every time you buzz yourself to oblivion."

I picture his amber stare, and this time I do feel a shiver. It's surprising but pleasant. It starts in my brain, trips down my spine, tingles lower.

"No?"

"You totally said that like it was a question."

Two hours later, I spill out of a cab. The rolling bag at my side and my backpack should have everything I'll need, but I feel naked.

I round the hotel to find two busses parked in the back, plus an eighteen-wheeler truck.

A woman sporting tailored jeans, heels, a cute blazer, and a blue Katy Perry ponytail comes up to me. "I'm Nina, the tour manager. You must be Haley. Shannon said we're adding one more here."

"That's me."

She tucks her tablet under her arm, presses her hands together, and executes a mini-bow. "Namaste."

"Um. Yeah, you too."

She straightens, and she's all business again. "Did you get the paperwork emailed to you?"

"I think so."

"Good. We're running late, but I can answer any questions you have once we get rolling."

She calls everyone's attention and goes over the schedule.

"We're off to Pittsburgh. Another sold-out show. We should get in by three. Curtain's at eight. It'll be a tight setup, but you've only done it fifty times."

A few people chuckle. The words bring a shiver over me as I look around the circle.

"All right, everyone get ready to roll out. Anyone seen Jerry?" Nina asks.

"Yeah. He's meeting us in Pittsburgh," a guy says.

She sighs. "Fine."

I still don't know who Jerry is, but everyone seems to want a piece of him today.

A striking redheaded woman who looks a few years older than me meets my gaze. "You must be the fresh meat."

"I'm Haley. And you're Lita Holm." I recognize her immediately. "You're opening for Jax. I loved your *Preacher* album."

"Not the new one?" She raises a brow, and I wince. "Don't take it back now. Honesty is refreshing." She doesn't offer me a hand. I like her already. "Come on. I'll show you around."

I shield my eyes from the sun with a hand, scanning the busses. "These are big."

"This one's for the crew and our band." She points at the other bus. "That one belongs to Riot Act. But rumor has it Mace, Kyle, and Brick get the front half. The rest is Jax's."

"Rumor?"

She raises a brow. "You think any of us see the inside?"

She nods toward the closer bus, and I get on, shouldering my bag.

"It's a pretty baller tour. We stay in hotels most nights." Relief courses through me. "Occasionally we have to travel overnight, and you can sleep here."

She gestures to the bunks at the back, and I take a slow breath.

I might not be able to sleep, but as long as it's not every night, it should be manageable.

A living room-type area makes up the front, and she drops onto a couch there.

"Tour rules." Her face gets serious as she holds

up fingers. "One, thou shalt shower every day. It seems obvious. Apparently it's not." She shoots a look at a guy who laughs. "Two, thou shalt not touch other people's shit."

"Three," a voice shouts from somewhere behind us, "thou shalt not beat Lita in her fantasy baseball league."

The woman in question flips him her middle finger before returning to me. "Not actually. Though I'd love to see you try. Three, thou shalt not fraternize with the crew or with the artists." I must look confused, because she says, "Fuck whoever you want as long as they're not on either of these busses. You'll get fired on the spot."

"That won't be an issue."

She shoots me a look. "You'd be surprised."

3

"**I**'m not interested in new opportunities. I don't give a shit how big the paycheck is."

I toss the phone, still uttering persuasive sounds, across the room and pick up my guitar instead.

My agent's nothing if not insistent. Thank God I don't pay him by the word.

My fingers pluck at the strings, and the knot in my gut lessens a degree.

Like most sicknesses, motion sickness is in your head. After ten years in the business, I can control it.

But lately, the low-grade discomfort of being on tour has grown into something bigger. Something unwieldy.

A sound like rain has me shifting on the

leather couch to see Mace's head sticking through the beaded curtain. "You working on something new?"

"You learn to knock?" I ask my guitarist.

He drops onto the couch across from mine. The back of my bus is bigger than the living room of the rent-controlled apartment I grew up in. I have nothing modern to compare it to since I've never bought myself a house.

"Wouldn't kill you to give the fans something," Mace says. "It's been a year."

He pops his gum because quitting smoking's a bitch and he won't let any of us forget it.

I play him the I-V-IV-V chord progression as I croon over the music. "I know a guy. His name is Mace. He likes to get fucked in the face..."

He bursts into laughter, the kind that shakes the bus. "Sounds like a hit."

The look in his eye when the laughter stops has my own smirk fading. "What've you been doing?"

"Nothing."

We've been friends long enough he knows not to lie to me. Alcohol's one thing, but I don't let shit on my tour. Not since the longest night of both our lives.

The night I made a contract with myself. Decided I'm responsible for everyone who works here, and I will do whatever I have to to keep them safe.

Mace shifts back on the couch. "What's happening with Jerry?"

"Nothing. He's the best goddamned sound tech in the country. He's been running shows since you were in diapers."

"Since my folks were, more like. He fucked up last week, Jax. Maybe the audience didn't notice, but it could've been a helluva lot worse. Next time..."

I silence him with a stare.

"Fine. Jerry's golden."

I'd stopped by the studio this morning to record an alternate version of a couple verses for an EP. I planned to get in, get out, and get on with my tour.

But the kid couldn't do his job, and Jerry was AWOL.

Then things had gone from annoying to X-Files weird when some unfamiliar girl shrieked at me in my own studio like I was forcing myself on her against the wall.

I can't remember a woman complaining about

me putting my hands on her before. And I'd barely touched her.

Had I overreacted by telling Cross to get rid of her?

Maybe. A thread of guilt tugs at my gut, but the brakes on the bus catch and I reach for the curtains. It's too soon to be in Pittsburgh.

I set down my guitar and follow Mace toward the front of the bus.

"Watch the Death Star," Mace warns. I skirt the half-built LEGO on the floor as I pass.

Brick looks up from the video game he's playing, and Kyle pockets his drumsticks.

Outside, I stalk toward the front of our convoy, brushing through the crew pulling off the other bus. Smoke billows from the front of the truck that holds all the equipment for the stage show.

"Pyro started early," Mace says.

Nina's already standing by the front, one hand on her hip and her brows fused together. The rest of the crew forms a half circle around the truck, standing at a safe distance.

Except one.

The girl in jeans and a leather jacket inches toward the front of the truck, craning her neck to see what the driver's doing over its open hood.

"Who's that?" Brick asks.

"They called her in to cover Jerry," Kyle says.

"Unbelievable," I mutter.

The remorse I might've felt about my role in getting her fired evaporates like sweat off hot asphalt at the realization that she's *not* fired.

It's twisted, sure. But if I gave myself shit for every twisted thought I have, I'd never find time to entertain millions of people.

Meaning no one here would have jobs.

So basically, cutting myself slack is great for the economy.

"Can we put all the equipment onto the bus?" Lita asks.

"It won't fit," Nina snaps, her gaze darting between the vehicles.

"What about your Zen shit, Neen?" Brick calls. "You always say we should live in the present."

"I'm in the present. It sucks."

Brick's laughter has her glaring.

"Looks like the fan belt," the driver says to her. "Need a replacement part."

"We don't have time. Twenty-thousand ticket holders expect to see this show in six hours."

The new girl crosses to the truck's passenger

door and runs a finger over the logo there. "What if you borrow one?"

"From where? We need this bus for the crew," Nina says.

"What about the other bus?"

Every pair of eyes turns to me.

"You mean *my* bus?"

"Jax, this is Haley," Nina murmurs almost as an afterthought. "It's not the worst idea. If the parts are compatible."

The driver shrugs. "Serpentine belts come in a few lengths. Got some tools in the back. I can check it out."

"It *is* the worst idea," I interrupt. "It's right up there with asbestos and "Gangnam Style." We're not leaving my bus at the side of the road and waiting for AAA."

The crew looks between us. Few people would go toe to toe with me and even fewer that I'd stick around long enough to argue with.

Nina squares her shoulders. "Jax, we have four hours of setup in Pittsburgh."

I don't want to leave the crew stuck, and she knows it. It's my name on the tour, but it's their livelihoods.

Nina closes the distance between us, her blue

eyes the same color as her hair. When she speaks, it's for my ears only. "You have two interviews before tonight's show. I know the full range of issues you have with this tour. But could you please assert yourself tomorrow?"

Nina's a pro, but I can see the panic under the edges.

I rub a hand over my neck, which is suddenly itching like a mother. I can already tell it's going to be one of those days.

"Fine," I decide. "Take what you need from under the hood, but I'm not leaving my bus."

"Thank you," Nina mouths before turning on her heel. "Mace, Kyle, Brick, on the crew bus. Haley, I have a new assignment for you. Make sure Jax gets to the venue."

She's gone before I can tell her that's not part of the deal.

Ninety minutes later, my band, my crew, and my instruments—save my favorite guitar—are pulling away down the road. My driver's tucked into the cab of the bus, reading a paper, and I pretend I wasn't just outsmarted by my three-time tour manager.

I ascend the stairs to my bus, cursing as I trip over Mace's LEGO at the top. I grab what's left of it and set it on the coffee table, including the little pieces.

No one tells you having a band's like having toddlers.

I shove the controllers off the couch, grab a seat cushion, and carry it back to the stairs.

I toss it at the surprised-looking girl standing at the bottom.

Problems come in all kinds of packages. Hers isn't the worst, which only annoys me more.

Her thick lashes are the same near-black as her hair. Her nose is small, like she'd have trouble wearing glasses. Her bottom lip's too big for the top one.

Under the leather jacket, she's got curves.

Not that I'm noticing.

"I bet you're pretty proud of yourself, huh? Let's get something straight," I say before she can respond. "I don't know why you're not fired. It's probably Cross' idea of a joke, sending you to babysit me. But until we get rescued by Navy SEALs or whoever gets dispatched to save our asses out here, you will sit right there"—I point to the shoulder—"while this inspired fucking plan of yours rolls out."

Without waiting for an answer, I shut the doors and retreat to the back of the bus.

My Emerson goes into its case. I grab some clothes from my built-in dresser and shove them in a duffel bag.

There are pictures pinned up around my bus, and I take one down and lay it inside the top of my bag.

I glance out the window. She's sitting on the dusty shoulder of the highway on her backpack, her computer open on her lap. Dust has collected on her faded jeans and Converse sneakers.

You never used to be such an asshole. The familiar female voice in my head comes out of nowhere.

Pain edges into my brain, and I glance down. My thumb's bleeding again. I rip off the piece of fingernail I've been tearing without noticing.

I suck on the spot where it stings, crossing to open the mini-fridge and grabbing two bottles of water with my other hand. I lower the window and toss one. It hits the ground next to the girl's knee, and she jumps.

I take a sip from mine, watching her through the half-open window. "Fuckturd."

She looks up, shielding her eyes from the sun. "Excuse me?"

I nod toward her computer. "The internet password."

She takes a drink of water before setting the bottle in the dust next to her. "T-U-R-D?"

"Yeah. How do they spell turd where you're from?"

I close the window without waiting for an answer and finish packing, then pull up a reality home reno program on my iPad. Nothing distracts me before a show like seeing a bunch of contractors argue over cellulose and spray foam for insulating a garage. It's blissful and mindless, which I need because in a couple of hours—assuming we ever make it to Pittsburgh—I'll be spun.

I drain my water and grab another. Before a show, I can drink Lake Michigan into the Sahara. I glance out the window to see if she needs one too, but she's gone.

"The fuck, babysitter..." I shoulder my guitar and my duffel and go outside to find a tow truck in front of us.

The man talking to the girl is scratching the

back of his neck. When she looks at her phone, he looks at her chest.

He's old enough to be her father and then some.

It's one thing for me to give her a hard time, but she's on my tour. I want to assume responsibility for this girl about as much as I want to adopt a special needs goldfish, but I didn't get the choice.

I step between them, feeling her move back immediately. I jerk my head toward the bus. "Get it to Wells Fargo by five."

If he recognizes me, he doesn't let on. "That's going to be hard, son."

I pull out my wallet, peel off three hundreds, and stuff them in the chest pocket of his stained shirt, right behind his name tag. "I have confidence in you, Mac."

A black limo pulls up, and I turn to the girl.

"Let's go, Curious George."

I go back to my bus to grab my duffel and, with a sigh, what's left of Mace's Death Star. I shouldn't care, but I have a spare hand and he's been building the thing all week.

I cross to the car and jerk the door open with unnecessary force. It takes me a second to realize she's reaching for the front door.

"In the back."

She hesitates, and I stare out the door at her.

"You coming?"

A moment later, she complies, dropping into the seat opposite.

There's lots of room in here for her, and me, and our bags, and more. But her gaze finds the toy on the seat next to me.

"It's Mace's," I explain. "He finished the Super Star Destroyer last week. It was a bitch to ship home. Bought him the *Ghostbusters* firehouse last year, and he never opened it. Says he's a purist."

"*Star Wars* only?"

"Apparently."

I study her.

Up close, I notice the dust on her jeans—and on her knees, through the ripped denim. It sticks to the cracks of her Converse. Only her hair, shiny and dark and hanging past her shoulders, seems to have escaped unharmed.

"You didn't notice how that guy was looking at you?" I comment.

Her gaze drops to her clothes. "Probably like I've been mining blood diamonds in the jungle."

The quick reply has me taking another look at her.

She's young, like me when I started in this business. Though now that she's not on the floor at my feet, she has control of herself.

Her face is oval. Fresh skin, as though she's never done drugs or even stayed up too late. Big brown eyes with a little green near the center. The kind of mouth PR people salivate over. If she were in this business, that mouth would spawn chatrooms and have millions of fanboys jerking off to her.

Curvy legs bump mine as she sets her backpack on the seat, and she jerks them back. Now they're tucked up comically tight in the spacious car.

"If you're worried I'm going to steal your virtue on the road to Pittsburgh," I drawl, "I don't fuck my employees." I frown. "I also don't fuck on back roads, but that's a personal choice."

She looks around for something—probably a seatbelt—then turns back to me when she comes up empty.

"I'm sorry about this morning. I shouldn't have shouted at you. Or hit you."

"Oh. You think?"

"You touched me," she goes on as if it explains anything.

"I *touched* you?" I raise my hands in the air. "You're still intact. Send word to the nuns."

Her gaze narrows. "I was startled."

"Yeah, me too."

I look out the window because at this rate, it's going to be a long fucking drive to Pittsburgh.

She pulls out her phone. If she's updating Cross already, I'm going to flip.

I lean forward and swipe it out of her hand.

The sound of protest low in her throat almost has me looking up again, but when I realize what's on the screen, I'm instantly preoccupied.

"You're editing a track?" I take a moment to read the dips and valleys, the graph that music is turned into by computers when it's dissected. "What's this app?"

"I made it." My gaze snaps to hers, and for the first time, I see confidence instead of uncertainty. "It uses research on how the human brain processes lyrics and music to adjust settings to maximize emotional resonance."

"Come again?"

She shifts so she's cross-legged, then inches closer so she can see the screen while she's talking. "Basically, it makes music that affects people. It's based on the assumption that music underscores lyrics. That we respond to both music and lyrics but the music is in service of the words. Words are the primary pathway. So I use this app to adjust musical arrangements to optimize the emotional resonance of the phrasing."

I stare at her.

She's not the first woman to do something crazy within seconds of meeting me. But she's the first to follow up with this. Whatever the hell this is.

I shake off the feeling of unease as I stretch my legs now that I have the entire space to work with. "Your assumption is wrong. The words are nothing without the music."

Instead of backing down, her expression sharpens with interest. "What about poetry?"

I cock my head. "What about it, babysitter?"

"It exists without music, but it touches people. Evokes a response."

Shit, she's committed to this idea.

Too bad I'm going to have to beat it into the ground.

"Even poetry has a meter. Besides, if words mattered so much, some of the best-known pieces of all time wouldn't be instrumental. Van Halen's "Eruption." Miles Davis' "Right Off." And don't get me started on Rush's "YYZ." The drum solo alone could level armies." I tap it out on my thigh with my free hand, and she listens.

When I finish, her attention flicks to the phone in my other hand, and I raise a brow. "You want it?"

The indecision on her face is comic gold, as if the idea of getting within a foot of me is horrifying.

Finally she leans forward, carefully plucking it from my hand and tucking it into the dusty backpack on the seat next to her.

I reach into my bag and pull out a chocolate bar.

"What is that?" she asks, her eyes widening as I unwrap it.

"Snickers. You're one of those health freaks too? Perfect."

"No. I have a peanut allergy. I almost died when I was four."

"So if I eat this thing in here..."

"You'll have to carry me out."

We stare at one another for a minute.

Two.

Finally, I buzz down the window and toss out the candy bar. She heaves a sigh of relief.

I grab a bottle of water from the bar. A piss-poor substitute for Snickers.

"Is this usually how you get to know your new employees?" she asks.

"Yes. It's part of a five-step process. Now tell me your dreams and fears. I'll take notes."

Her eyes glint. "My dreams? I want to do something that matters to the world. And I'm afraid of dying of anaphylactic shock in a limo with a rock star."

I reach for Mace's toy sphere. It's done enough to have shape, but some of the decorations are missing. I lift it, turning it in my hands as I look at her through the gaps. "Death scares you. That's healthy."

"Not dying exactly. More like making twenty thousand Pittsburgh music fans curse my immortal soul."

Normally my first impressions are spot on. But maybe—just maybe—I was a little off on this girl.

You can't blame me. Thousands of bright-eyed kids want to be me, to get close to me.

Now that we're flying down the highway in the back of a limo and not in a studio, she's not awed at all.

I set the sphere in my lap. "So, what? You're going to tell computers what to do for the rest of your life?"

"I'm pretty good at it. It's a solid career path."

I'm shaking my head before she finishes.

"Going with the flow is insidious. You'll be an animal, driven by whatever master exerts himself on you."

"But people *are* animals," she responds easily. "We live. We die. Somewhere in between, we procreate."

"Not if the nuns have their say," I say drily.

She levels me with a look. "Come on. Nuns are secretly fans of procreation. Even if they don't practice it. Otherwise there'd never be any new nuns." I swallow the laugh, but she keeps going. "Do you like animals?"

I lift two LEGO Jedi from the spots they're plugged into, turning them in my hands so their lightsabers clash.

"Not like Kyle. I see the kid on one more SPCA commercial, I'm going to shoot myself in the head. But Shark Week's still a classic."

Her eyes light up. "Have you seen the documentary *Planet Earth*?"

"Nope."

"It's insane. They use a combination of cameramen plus all of this technology to shoot footage of animals in remote areas no humans would be able to get to. In one episode about jungles, there's this jaguar that stalks the rivers and eats—"

"Whoa." I raise a hand. "Didn't anybody tell you tour rules?"

She straightens. "I got three."

"Rule twelve: no spoilers on tour."

"It's nature. You can't spoil nature." Then she pauses. "How many rules are there?"

"A lot."

"Does the fact that you don't want me to spoil it mean you're going to watch it?"

I shoot her a smirk. "I'm Jax Jamieson, babysitter. I don't have time to watch documentaries."

I plug the Jedi back onto their spots and set the toy next to me. Then I close my eyes, tapping a finger along the armrest.

Tap-tap, tap-tap, tap-tap.

Eventually, I pry open one eyelid to see her still watching me.

"Netflix or Hulu?"

4

HALEY

They say don't meet your heroes.

For a moment this afternoon, I'd thought mine was going to leave me to die by the side of the road.

So, we didn't get off to the best start. But when I caught him looking at the track on my phone, it was like the judgement fell away and a light went on. He studied the dips and valleys, the frequencies that together made the sounds.

When Jax's eyes closed, I tried to write an email to let Professor Carter know about my internship. We only have a few weeks left to finalize my Spark competition submission, and we'll have to do it by email.

I couldn't focus, and it wasn't the motion of the spacious car cruising down the interstate or the growling of my stomach after realizing I hadn't had lunch today.

It was because I was being a girl.

Sneaking looks at Jax.

How a guy pulls off looking manly while holding a LEGO set, I'll never know.

Serena would've winked if she'd been in the car.

When Jax and I roll into Pittsburgh, he's swept away for interviews by a determined Nina, leaving me to find the elusive Jerry.

The empty arena is a cavernous testament to technology and scale and the demands of mankind to be entertained.

The sound booth is at the back and midway up the rows of seats. It has a killer view of the stage. Even with twenty thousand people, it will. That thought sends chills running through me.

I stand behind the board. It's a mix of old and new. Mechanical and digital. A wall of computer screens interfaces with the switches and dials.

I feel even more out of my element than before.

"Billy Joel."

I jump at the raspy voice behind me. Its owner's hunched shoulders make him look even older, and shorter, than he really is. The man is stocky, wearing a faded black T-shirt and black jeans. His face is faded too and lined. But the blue eyes set between the creases are clear.

"The first concert I did here. Billy Joel."

"It must have been incredible. I'm Haley. You must be Jerry."

His nod is more like a bob. His hands look like crumpled paper. Rough on the surface, fragile underneath.

"You're my new assistant." He says it with a dry chuckle. I wait for him to strip me down, tell me I'm not needed or wanted, but all he does is scratch a patch of silver hair on his head. "You ever used a board like this?"

"No. I mostly use a DAW. Started on Logic, moved to Ableton."

He makes a face. "Digital. This handles more than a hundred tracks. Twelve for drums alone."

My gaze runs over the board. For the first time since this morning, I feel something flirting with my consciousness.

Comprehension. Just out of reach but nearer than it's been during this crazy day.

"No backup tracks?"

"Everything is live. Every drum beat, every guitar riff comes from that stage and through here." He reaches out to tap the board, his red plaid shirt following the movement.

He tells me a series of numbers for the guitars, mic, bass, which I commit to memory.

"What about the opening act?" I ask.

"What about them?"

"I met five musicians on the bus. We have Lita"—I point at the board—"her guitarist, bassist, drums. Where're her keys?"

Jerry shifts over to make room, then talks me through the specs sheet of the equipment we're using. Frequency response, SPL output, dispersion.

I know all the terms, but I've never seen the equal of this equipment. I try to absorb all of it, my brain firing on every cylinder.

Part of me wonders if I should make notes, but I'm more of a visual person, so I try to soak up every piece of the desk that looks like it could fly the Enterprise.

Not the Kirk version. Definitely the Picard one.

Maybe even Archer.

"Help me with those cords, will you?"

I reach over to where he's pointing and start removing zip ties from the equipment. "So how do you know how to get the right sound in a venue? Is it based solely on the specs, or do you talk to other sound engineers?"

I pull up a window on my phone to look for venue info, but he holds up a hand. "I've mixed thirty shows in Wells Fargo."

I lower the phone, slow.

Jerry shifts back against the low wall that separates the booth from the surrounding seats, his arms folding over his thick chest. For a second I wonder if he's forgotten about me. But he says, "I have an idea. Watch tonight from up there." He points at the stage.

"Backstage?"

"To know what's working, you need to see the audience. That's your job tonight—to watch."

Shit. I think I might be having a cardiac arrest.

I'm too young to die of a heart attack. But then, it's too much to ask me to internalize the excitement of watching a Jax Jamieson show from backstage.

On stage, the roadies are setting up, along with the lighting techs and the guitar and keyboard techs. It's orchestrated chaos. Some of it will be for the opening act, but most of it's for the main event.

The next hour flies by in last-minute fixes

before I'm pushed backstage as the fans fill the space.

All of it transfixes me. The setup is completed with a jerky efficiency, but it might as well be the finest ballet.

Lita's band plays first, and I'm hypnotized. She's really damn good. I watch her get her final applause and unplug her guitar.

Once the curtain falls, the crew takes over. Unplugging and plugging cords. Rearranging equipment.

"You lost, babysitter?"

The one-in-a-million voice has me turning to find Jax behind me for the second time today.

This time, I should be prepared.

You're so not.

He's dressed in black from head to toe. His body is hard and lean and sculpted, and I wish I could pull a Dr. Strange just to freeze time and check out every muscle one by one.

His hair's got some kind of product in it, and I'm pretty sure he has stage makeup on.

Those amber eyes are the same.

I always thought Jax Jamieson gutted people with his voice. I'm starting to think he could do it with that stare alone.

"Jerry said I could watch from up here," I say.

"Did he?"

I'm getting better at not melting into a pile of stuttering goop when he challenges me. It's something I'll have to practice if I'm going to be here for a month.

On stage, the crew is finishing up. Kyle takes his spot behind the drums, doing a visual check. Brick sets up behind his bass on the far side of the stage. Mace leaves his guitar unplugged as his fingers warm up over the strings. He's muttering to himself.

"He okay?" I ask.

"He'll survive. But apparently Emperor Palpatine's throne broke off and went AWOL in transit today."

I remember the Death Star that'd ridden along with us. "Crap. And he blames it on you."

"Nah. I told him it was your fault."

My jaw drops. "Why would you do that?"

"Man doesn't get his Snickers, he's bound to do some crazy shit." Jax strides past me, shaking his head as he takes the stage.

Was that a joke? I remember from a media interview that he's supposed to have a dry sense of humor, but right now I'm not sure.

Still, I can't take my eyes off him as he lifts his guitar from its rack, shifting it over his head with the easy grace of someone who does it as effortlessly as walking.

My skin's tingling everywhere. Not in a bad way, a good one.

The crowd can't even see him yet, and they're going crazy in the darkness.

He's in his own world. Walking a slow circle, his eyes closed, he stops in front of the mic, dropping his head back.

He could be a Western gunslinger or a gladiator. The confidence. The competence.

Then the curtain rises.

The venue explodes, the roar filling my ears.

Jax looks immune, but when he lifts his head, opens his eyes, the roar gets louder.

The sea of people is marked by grins and bouncing and excitement.

But like yesterday in the interview room, my attention drags back to the man on the stage.

Jax's profile is in sharp relief, his strong nose and chin outlined against the powerful stage lights.

There's no music, no talking, just screaming that takes a moment to fade.

When it does, the arena is quiet.

Jax shifts imperceptibly closer to the mic stand. His gaze drops to the big, square mic as though he can see inside it. As though he knows every inch of it well enough to recreate it in his mind.

It's a million degrees next to the stage, but my arms are pebbled with goose bumps.

His lips part, his chest rising. He's the only one breathing in the entire venue.

And then...

A single note, low and raw, splits the silence.

The tension shatters. The quiet too, as twenty thousand people recognize the hit song and erupt into cheers.

My lips fall open, but I can't hear any sound that comes out.

I'm reminded in an instant why Jax Jamieson's a damned magician.

Not because his songs are perfect. Because they're *real*.

The program I'm building can't explain the kind of genius this man brings when he writes a song.

But every line, every verse, every chord touches me like nothing else does. The vibration fills me, owns me, in a way no person ever has.

It takes a moment to realize Nina's next to me, looking relaxed for the first time since the truck broke down.

"It's not always easy," she comments, the beatific smile making her look more like a Dove commercial than a tour manager. "But in these moments? It's worth it."

5

HALEY

Dear Professor Carter,

I wanted to let you know that I've accepted a position with a music recording company for the summer. I'm sorry we aren't able to work together, as that would have been amazing, but I hope I can continue to count on your advice as I prepare my program for the Spark competition. Thanks again for agreeing to serve as a sponsor for my application.

Sincerely,

Haley

My phone rings and I reach across the bed for it. "Hey."

"Bitch. You didn't call me last night."

"I was working."

"Chain smoking too?"

I crack a grin and shift upright to stare at the clock. Seven thirty.

"You're up early," Serena says.

"You too. I'm emailing Professor Carter. What sounds more personal: sincerely or yours truly?"

"How about 'I get off to you every night'?"

I make a face, hit Send, and shut my laptop as I slide out of bed.

"I didn't call to hear about Carter. How was it last night?"

"I got to bed at two."

"Partying like a rock star."

"Not partying. Going over the settings and cues with a guy who could be my grandfather." After the show, Jerry had wanted to see what I'd noticed, so I'd gone back to the sound booth and spent an hour with him, talking and taking notes.

I go through my bag for clean socks in the bottom.

My fingers close on...

"You snuck condoms in my bag?" I hold one up, my voice incredulous.

"Better safe than sorry," she chirps.

I drop the box back in the bag, shaking my head. "I did sleep in a hotel last night. Alone."

Besides Lita and Nina, I'm the only woman on tour, which apparently means I get my own room.

"Lucky. Need a roommate on the road?"

I yawn and stretch. "I don't think any pets are allowed. And Scrunchie is an especially tough sell." I shift out of bed, peering out the curtains to see the sunlight.

"Something came in the mail today. I think it's the ancestry test."

My spine straightens. "Open it."

I hear her rustling in the background and wait, dragging my sock-covered toe against the baseboard.

"Well?"

"No relatives found." I drop the curtain, my stomach flip-flopping. "I'm sorry, Haley."

"It's okay. I knew there wasn't a good chance. But it's actually not that bad. Maybe it's not meant to be. I never felt like I was missing out by not knowing who my father is. Maybe he doesn't even know about me. That would be one hell of a surprise. Or he could be in jail for all I know."

"Your mom doesn't strike me as the type."

"I don't know what her type was. I never really saw her with a man." I wander into the bathroom, inspecting the little toiletries there. I guess even nice hotels have crappy shampoo, and I'm glad I brought my own. "I know it shouldn't change anything, adding a face and a name to my family tree. Even if it's more like a family shrub."

There's a little pot for coffee, and I wrinkle my nose as I follow the instructions, pouring water into the reservoir and hitting the button.

"I want to find out who I am. But maybe that's what this month is about. Maybe I can find myself here."

I glance in the mirror opposite the bed.

"Knowing your parents isn't all its cracked up to be. My dad asked me whether companies record video chats."

"What? Why?"

"Because he's doing shit I don't want to know about with some yoga instructor."

"Oh, gross. I don't want to hear about your dad's sex life."

"Me either. Let's talk about mine. Did I

mention Declan from my finance class asked me out?"

The water boils, sending up a plume of steam from the plastic coffee maker.

"That was last week."

"No, that was Nolan from my media class."

I drop onto the bed with my black coffee cupped in my hands and listen to my friend on speakerphone. She tells me about all the guys she has wound around her finger, which makes me feel more at home and miss it at once.

Even if I'm never going to have the kind of confidence with guys that she does, will never crave physical contact the same way? I like hearing about it.

Eventually, we hang up.

Surprisingly—or maybe not—no one else is in the hall after I shower and get dressed in comfy jeans, a soft bra and a white cotton T-shirt that skims my boobs and hips. My leather jacket goes overtop.

I don't know what the breakfast situation is, if we can charge it to our room or what, so I stick to coffee from the continental breakfast laid out in the hallway.

I work on my program, thinking about what Jax said about music and lyrics.

Maybe when I'm done preparing for Spark, I can run some alternative models with instrumental songs. See if I can hack those too.

Lita comes downstairs after ten in skinny jeans, a long-sleeved T-shirt and sandals. Her hair's piled up on her head, and she looks like a sleepy ballerina. "New girl. Come with me."

I pack up my laptop. "Where is everyone?"

"Half of them are already at the venue, and the other half are still in bed."

Lita doesn't seem to have the same concerns about ordering breakfast. A waiter delivers two eggs and three pieces of bacon to the table in front of her.

Over breakfast, she explains what to expect. "When we're doing back-to-back shows in a town, the setup's not too bad. Most of the day's filled up with media. Then sound check. Rehearsal if there's time."

"Do you have time to communicate with the outside world?"

"Unless the outside world has a ticket to that night's show? Not usually."

I turn that over in my mind. "It must be hard. What about people's boyfriends? Girlfriends?"

"They understand. Or they don't." She smirks. "I'm unattached. I like it that way. My band is too."

"What about Riot Act?"

"Mace only cares about music. Kyle loves all women. Brick? You'll hear soon enough."

"And Jax?" I try for casual.

I don't succeed.

Lita grins, a sparkle in her eye. "Don't go there, new girl. Trust me."

We ride over to the venue together with a couple of her bandmates. Nina and Jax have apparently been in interviews for hours already.

On the way over, she pulls out her phone and starts cursing.

"What's wrong?" I ask.

Lita's bassist grins. "We're thirty days into baseball season, and her second baseman's already on the DL."

I hide the smile. "What do you like about fantasy sports? Is it the competition?"

Lita lifts her gaze from the screen. "It's no competition, new girl. If I wasn't already employed as a musician, I'd make the best owner in baseball."

When I get to the sound booth, I see the familiar setup from last night.

What I don't see is Jerry.

I use the time to go over the desk, the program. I try to match up the settings with what I saw backstage. I go over the specs for this stop, start on the ones for our next stop. My running list of questions gets inputted to my phone.

Still no Jerry.

I sneak an hour working on my program while I wait.

Eventually I look up to find him shuffling down the aisle toward the booth. Today's plaid shirt is green.

He grunts when he sees me. "What are you doing here?"

"Um. You told me to meet you here at one." I check my watch. It's nearly three.

Instead of explaining, he scoffs. "You're keeping tabs on me."

"I'm your assistant."

"If you were my assistant, you'd do what I say." His voice sharpens. "Now don't touch that and leave me to do my damned job."

He shoves past me.

I stare after him as he hunches over the desk in front of the computer.

I'm used to people being protective of their work, but this is something else.

How am I supposed to assist Jerry if he won't let me in the sound booth? I sense there's something bigger going on here but have no idea what it is.

What is obvious is that everyone else at the venue is occupied with their own work. Nina's nowhere in sight. Security's busy.

I go backstage to try to figure out what I should do.

Nina's voice comes from the open door at the end of the hall. "We'll find it later."

"No. We'll find it *now*." The growl echoes off the walls.

My spine stiffens as I stop in front of the doorway. It looks like a tornado hit. The room is full of scattered costumes, equipment, and food.

Jax grabs an amp off the floor and hurls it across the room. I jump as it hits the wall.

Finally he stops spinning, his eyes wild as our gazes lock. I look from him to Nina, who's talking into her phone, and back.

"Where is it?" he demands.

"What?"

I look around because why is he suddenly talking only to me?

"My *phone*, babysitter," he says it as though I'm purposely keeping it from him.

"I… when did you lose it?"

"If I knew that, I'd have it right now," he grinds out.

Nina's running down their itinerary from earlier, calling every studio they interviewed at.

I can't remember seeing the phone in the limo or during any of our time together. "Did you leave it on your bus?"

"Not possible," he mutters, stalking past me.

I follow him into the hall. Jax rubs a hand over his head, sending the muscles under his tight T-shirt leaping.

Yesterday he was irritated, but I'd figured it was just edginess before the show.

Now, he's not edgy. He's volatile.

"We'll find it after the show." Nina's calm voice cuts in from behind us.

"No, Nina, we will *not* find it after the show. There will not *be* a fucking show."

Kyle sticks his head out the door. Of Jax's band

members, he seems the most approachable, looking as if he could be a grad student.

"He has a password on it, right?" I ask.

"It's not about privacy. He needs to make a call tonight."

I stare. "Can't he borrow a phone? All phones reach all other phones. That's how phones work."

"It's a long story."

The feeling stirring up inside me should be annoyance. But as I watch Jax rub a hand over his neck, eyes wild, the only thing I feel is concern.

I check the clock. The opening act goes on in an hour.

You need to get back to the sound booth, a voice reminds me. *Figure out how to do the job you were given.*

Instead, I reach for my phone and slip out the door.

———

"It's me, Haley. I called about the bus."

The man at the auto shop, Mac, looks the same as yesterday. "You want on it."

"Yes." I flash him my ID. I remember Jax's

comment, and a ripple of uncertainty runs through me. Maybe this wasn't a good idea.

"Wicked Records, right? It's not ready. Work order says it'll be done tomorrow morning."

"I need to get onto it now."

For a moment, he blinks. Then he looks past me toward the door, like he's wondering if someone else is with me.

Of course, I'm alone.

Which I'm starting to think was a dumb idea.

His gaze drops down my body, then back up. He sneers. "What'll you do for me?"

I can hear Serena's voice telling me to kick him in the balls or something.

"What I'll do is tell management at Wicked Records how cooperative you were." I force myself to stand my ground. "Now can I get on the bus?"

The front of the bus is leather and glass. Couches on both sides, a chandelier on the ceiling. Gaming controllers are scattered across the couch cushions. It smells faintly of cigarettes, as if someone used to smoke here.

When I brush through a beaded curtain, I'm in Jax's world.

Everything is dark red. The walls are covered in photos of a woman with a sweet face. A kid. In some pictures, they're with Jax, his arm around them. He's grinning like he's won the lottery.

Is he married? A father?

None of that has ever been reported in the media.

That's not why you're here, I remind myself, though it feels like the world's been turned inside out in the last few seconds.

It takes me a couple of minutes to find what I'm looking for because it's tucked under the edge of the couch.

"Holy shit. Is this it?" I hold up the flip phone.

Creaking behind me has me stumbling upright. Ty's coming on the bus.

"You find what you need?" he asks, leering. He moves toward me, and an alarm sounds in the back of my mind.

He doesn't look like he wants to touch me in that benevolent, annoying way society seems to permit.

He looks as if he wants to do a whole lot more than that.

"Mac," I whisper. "Please don't touch me."

"Someone going to have a problem with that?"

I hold my breath because no.

No one's going to have a problem with it.

No one knows I'm here.

He reaches for me, and my heart kicks in my chest.

I twist away.

He catches hold of my jacket, and I use the chance to wriggle free.

I duck under his arm. The phone and charger in tow, I race out of the bus.

My jacket! part of me protests.

But I run and keep running.

The car I took over here picks me up, and somewhere on the drive back to the arena, I hit the power button.

The phone has messages from someone named Annie. The woman in the photos?

Where are you?

When I get back to the backstage door, the guards have changed and they stare me down.

"I work here, I swear." I reach for my ID, but I can't find it. I hope to hell I didn't leave it at the garage...

"Nina! Jax!" The words are hollered at the top of my lungs.

The security guy goes for me, and I back up.

Through the crack in the door, I see Jax burst through the door partway down the hall, but before I can say anything, the door shuts in my face.

Shit.

A moment later the door opens. A breath whooshes out of my lungs as I brush past the security guard and toward Jax.

His notices the phone in my hand, and his shoulders relax. "Where did you find this?"

"Your bus." I hand Jax the phone and dig the charger out of my bag. "I figured no one else would be able to charge... whatever that is."

Jax studies me as if he's trying to decide what I'm made of on a cellular level.

"Thanks, babysitter," he says finally.

He turns and starts toward the stage door.

"My name is Haley," I call after him. Jax pauses, hesitation only noticeable because I'm watching him so closely, then keeps walking.

The last hour catches up to me, the fact that I hauled my ass across town to bargain with some guy who clearly likes his girls younger than half his age plus seven.

I lost my jacket, all for some ten-year-old piece-of-shit handset that doesn't even matter. I squeeze my hands into fists.

Maybe Serena's right.

Not just about the sex part, but that Jax Jamieson's not someone I can learn from. He shouldn't be on a pedestal.

He's talented, but he's also self-centered.

He goes through life with people throwing themselves at his feet.

People like that lose touch with what it's like to be human. They don't remember what it's like to need other people. They can act however they want and do whatever they want because the world caters to them.

I take a minute to rub my hands over my face, then start toward the backstage door.

When I pass through the doorway, my eyes adjusting to the dark beyond, I pull up.

Jax is on the phone, his face transformed from earlier. I can't hear what he's saying, but the way he says it is caring. Like the man in the photos.

He's leaning forward, and his mouth curves at

the corner. When he rubs a hand over his neck, the tattoos on his biceps leap.

There's none of the cockiness that's part of his persona onstage. He's just a guy.

Jax isn't acting for the fans or the paparazzi or anyone. He's basically alone, or as close as you can get backstage at a rock concert.

And he's lit up like a Christmas tree.

My chest squeezes because it's beautiful to watch. I move closer in the dark.

I don't realize I'm blocking the way until one of the crew brushes past me.

I inch closer to the stage with a muttered apology that won't be heard over the sound of Lita and her band less than twenty yards away.

When I glance back up, Jax is pocketing the phone.

"If that rings while you're out there..." Nina warns.

I brace for an explosion, but Jax is a different person. He ruffles her hair, and she ducks away with a reluctant grin.

I don't realize I'm staring until Jax's gaze levels on me.

Shit.

I'm definitely in the wrong here. Not because I shouldn't be backstage because, hello, I work here.

More because I feel like I witnessed a moment that wasn't mine to see.

I start to turn, but Jax is walking toward me. It's too late.

"Do me a favor," he says when he pulls up.

His body's bigger than I remember, his hard chest inches from my face.

I force myself to breathe as if he's not close enough to encircle me with his arms.

My hips are yanked forward as if by an invisible cord, and it takes a second to realize it's his finger in my belt loop.

Holy shit.

"Hang onto this for me. *Haley*." His voice rumbles over the applause on the other side of the curtain.

My mouth falls open on a gasp as the phone slides inside the front pocket of my jeans, wedging in the narrow opening and creating friction everywhere it touches.

I'm not used to shaking hands with strangers, but right now, I feel his touch somewhere I never expected a rock star's *anything* to get near in my lifetime.

Ripples of sensation shoot down my spine, between my thighs.

Jax's grin is long gone, and as his amber stare bores into me, I swear he knows exactly what he's doing.

My skin burns like the phone is hot. Part of me wants to yank the thing out and toss it across the floor.

Instead, as I watch him take the stage, I press my palm over my pocket so the outline digs into my hip.

"You ever going to play a cover?" Lita calls over the muffled shuffling of feet on the hotel's carpeted lobby floor as we wait for elevators. The overhead lights cast a harsh glow on artists and crew alike, all holding the same energy of excitement and exhaustion. "They loved our Cranberries song."

"Not going to happen," Jax says. "I don't do other people's shit."

"What about 'Inside'? That's *your* shit. From another lifetime." Mace says it like a joke as we pile onto two elevators.

I'm swept into the one with Lita, Nina, Jax, Mace, and their drummer Kyle, plus a couple of the techs whose names I'm still learning.

"Would it kill you to play it for your fans?"

Nina glances up from her phone, looking as alert as she did at noon even though it's after midnight.

"It might."

The doors start to close, then hesitate.

"I'll get the next one." I start to step out, but Lita sticks her arm in front of me.

"Don't be dumb. If you haven't figured it out, personal space doesn't exist here."

Tour rule number twenty-three: no one is content to live in their own bubble; they need to bust uninvited into yours as well.

Disliking being touched by strangers should largely go unnoticed in life, but you'd be surprised how many times it comes up.

Everywhere from café lines to house parties to movie theatres.

By far the worst offender is elevators.

"Kyle, you have to stop giving shout-outs to random charities." This is Nina's voice.

"We're lucky to be famous, Neen," the drummer replies easily. "We should use that making the world a better place."

"We need to scope them before we tell your fans to give their money to the *Coalition for Panda Feelings*. That is not a real organization."

As the doors close again, my feet inch back until I'm pressed against a hard chest.

I know without looking who it is. I feel the sweat through his shirt, smell the salt.

"I'm going to start a charity," Brick drawls. "The *Free Blowjob Society*." Everyone groans. "You tell me that's not making the world a better place, you're full of shit."

I try to move, but there's nowhere to go. I turn my head, and my ponytail bumps something. Probably Jax's face, I realize as Brick stifles a laugh.

"Sorry." I face forward again.

"How did you like the show, Haley?" Mace asks.

"It was, ah"—Jax's chest rubs my back as he shifts—"loud. I mean... good."

After Jax slipped me the phone, I'd found my way back to the sound booth.

Jerry had acted as if he'd never tried to get rid of me earlier, even berating me for being late.

I couldn't get a handle on it.

I can't get a handle on a lot of things.

"Good?" Mace glances in amusement between me and the man behind me. "I think that's the first 'good' we ever got, Jax."

I'm counting the floors in this tiny box rising through the air.

Being in a confined space with lots of sensory stimulation makes me want to crawl out of my skin. Now, there's the buzz of chatter, the faint scent of sweat and makeup. A breath at my ear cuts through the rest, sending shivers down my spine.

The elevator dings, and I burst out first.

The hallway feels as open as the Grand Canyon, and I suck in fresh air.

"I thought we had the entire floor?" I ask Lita, nodding toward the open door at the end of the hall. Loud music and female laughter pour out of it.

"We do."

"Incoming!" Kyle hollers as he and Mace bound toward the room.

A woman sticks her head out, grinning and holding up a bottle of tequila. "About time!"

It clicks for me even before Nina warns, "Get a good night's sleep. The busses will be ready to roll out at ten."

Brick darts past Nina, turning to salute her with a mocking grin. Jax trails a few paces behind.

The band and crew disperse down the hall to their rooms, like pool balls after the break.

But I'm focused on one particular back.

"Do they do this every night?" I ask, staring after the band.

Lita doesn't respond, and I turn back to find her sympathetic gaze on me.

"Rule number thirty: don't."

"Don't what?"

"Don't ask. Don't wonder. Don't think about going down there. After having twenty thousand fans scream their names, they're all kinds of spun." With a wink, she vanishes into her room.

They're all kinds of spun.

The image of Jax talking to Annie on the phone flashes across my mind.

I read my room number off the card and pad down the hall to the second door opposite the elevator. I drop my duffel and swipe the key over the pad, making the light go green.

"What's your deal?" My head jerks up to see Jax standing outside the door at the end of the hall. "You practically sprinted off the elevator. You holding something against me?"

I blow out a breath. "Touching strangers weirds me out."

I didn't mean for it to be a conversation starter, but he strolls closer, the lights on the walls casting a bronze glow on his face.

He changed T-shirts after the show, and I wish he'd put on more because my gaze is drawn to the ink on his muscled arm.

"My mom tried to send me to daycare when I was three," I go on, looking for something to say that's not about his biceps. "Apparently I kicked an open bottle of finger paint at the woman who ran it when she tried to put an apron on me. After that, she put me in my own corner. Not great for social skills."

He pulls up right in front of me. "Some days it feels like all I do is have strangers touch me."

I wrap my arms around myself, shivering. "Sounds like my hell."

A ghost of a smile crosses his face, but it's gone so fast I might be wrong. "You get used to it. Or maybe you don't." He shrugs, though the look in his eye is anything but casual. "Anyone gives you a hard time, come to me."

The protectiveness in his voice is unexpected. "I can take care of myself."

"Never said you couldn't. But you're on my tour. Your job is to look out for me. Least I can do is look out for you."

I never thought of it that way. "Okay. Thanks."

His gaze drops down my body. When it drags

back up, I realize Lita's right—he does look spun. "I need something from you."

Jax nods to my jeans, and I think my airway closes. It takes a long second for my brain to click into gear. "Oh!"

I dig in my pocket for the phone and hold it out.

He takes it from me, careful not to let our fingers brush, and I'm sure it's on purpose.

"Why do you have a flip phone," I blurt as he tucks the device in his pocket.

"To remember where I come from."

"2007?"

My comment earns me a slow grin that sends tingles all the way to my toes.

The smile freezes on my face when I hear a door open down the hall. One of Lita's band members emerges, ice bucket in hand. He waves in greeting, then continues past us toward the ice room, which, judging by the sign, is at the end of the hall.

I'm suddenly aware it's just two of us in this hallway.

I shove my hands in my back pockets. "Well, I should get to sleep, or I'm not going to retain the ten million things Jerry told me."

"Wait." Jax's voice has me stilling, and for a second I wonder if he doesn't want to leave either. "Who was better than me."

He's talking about the show. He has to be.

Though now that he's so close, his amber eyes glinting with challenge, I want to say, "No one's better," because how could they be? At anything?

He's intense and beautiful and unlike even the prettiest of the pretty boys Serena brings through our house. Jax is different.

He's not a boy. He's a man.

He's a legend.

"Leonard Cohen," I whisper. "Radio City Music Hall. He was eighty."

His frown softens into confusion. "I'm competing with an eighty-year-old man?"

"He was forced to tour when his money was mismanaged and ran out. He started out with Canadian dates but ended up selling out all over the world, and... never mind."

The guy from Lita's band makes his return journey down the hall, and I step back on instinct because I'm pretty sure the space between us is short of professional.

"Haley," Jax murmurs when the door down the

hall closes. His lips are parted. His hair is still sweaty from the show. He needs a shower.

Judging from the tingling at the base of my spine, I might too.

"I know who Leonard fucking Cohen is." Jax's words drag me back. "I saw him at the Orpheum in Memphis."

I blink. The smile's faded, but there's still amusement in his eyes. "Oh my God. I've always wanted to see a show at the Orpheum. Was it incredible?"

Laughter sounds from down the hall, but I don't turn until the woman's voice shrieks, "Jax!"

I jump a mile, and both Jax's head and mine jerk toward the party room at the end.

A blond woman in a tube top and the smallest shorts I've ever seen spills out of the door.

And also the tube top.

"Get your hot ass down here!" Her voice is full of intention and attention, and there's no question what she wants to do with his hot ass.

That's when I realize there's a hand on my hip.

Jax's hand.

I glance down at it, and he does too.

He drops me.

For a second, I resent the fact that Jax Jamieson

is beloved the world over, because it means everyone wants a piece of him.

And there's only one of him to go around.

Jax turns back to me, and I imagine there's indecision in his gaze.

I'm willing to bet the woman down the hall doesn't want to talk about the Orpheum. Or probably talk at all.

"I bet there's a Snickers waiting for you down the hall," I offer. "She'd probably even unwrap it for you."

He rubs a hand over his neck, and I swallow at the way the ink moves across his arm as he flexes. "No doubt." Jax tosses his hair out of his face. "Sleep well, babysitter," he murmurs.

Then turns and walks back down the hall toward the Den of Sin.

7

People who haven't been on tour think it's basically like living in *The Hangover*.

Booze. Drugs. Strippers.

Tigers.

Zach Galifianakis wandering through the background in his underwear.

It's not true.

The scene around me tonight, though, is pretty cliché.

"Jax, baby, come on." The blonde shifts onto my lap, wiggling to get there. Her mouth pouts with whatever gloss she slicked on while she was thinking about me, or Brick, or Kyle, or Mace. Most of them don't care which.

Right now, I'm a hard pass.

It's been a long time since I screwed around on tour, and almost as long since I've wanted to.

I shift out from underneath her and reach into my pocket for the device I'm suddenly more protective of. I bang out a text.

Need 2 take my mnd off thgs

I glance at Mace, who's making out with a brunette. I'd never hear the end of it if he knew what I was doing.

At the bar across the room, I fix myself a bourbon because I like the way it makes my throat curl inward after a long night of spilling my guts into the mic.

Kyle and two redheads who look like twins are dueling on *Guitar Hero* in the next room.

Brick is plugged into a console in the corner playing *Fortnite*.

The only woman he even looks at is Nina, and I'd know if something happened there. Even if one of them wasn't too proud to admit it, neither of them would break the rules.

I can imagine it's a shitty place to be. When the person you want's the one person you can't have.

The drink's gone, and still my phone's silent. I send another message.

Where r u?

I slip out of the band's room and into my suite at the end of the hall. My bags are there, still zipped up.

The first week of tour, some assistant's assistant tried to unpack for me. It didn't end well.

On top is a stack of paper, different sizes, held together with a clip.

I could try to write—a phrase, a verse, a bridge —but I haven't turned out a good song in years. I'm not just losing my edge—I've lost it.

I pull my phone from my pocket and drop it on the bed. I strip the shirt over my head, wincing as I do. The mirror reveals a bruise near my rib, and I don't know how I got it.

I strip off my jeans, dropping them and my shirt in a pile in the corner of the room. My shorts go next.

The shower's hot and welcoming as I soap off the sweat, the grime, the makeup.

I let my mind go blank. For all of Neen's obsession with Buddhist monks or whatever, there's something to be said for living in the moment. It gives you relief from your thoughts.

One thought drifts through my mind and refuses to let go.

Leonard fucking Cohen.

The girl knows music, I'll give her that.

I'm tempted to ask Nina where Haley came from, but knowing the background of every tech on my tour is definitely below my paygrade.

I'm curious. That's all.

Maybe because she's the opposite of everyone else around here. The women who want to strip naked and do anything I ask.

I don't judge them. It's part of the aura, the sheen.

I have a halo around my head that's as fake as the rest of this circus.

But I get it. They don't really want me. They want the circus.

Haley on the other hand...

Being close to me physically seems to sicken her.

Though when I'd grabbed her hip—a reflex when she jumped at the sudden noise down the hall—she hadn't screamed.

Or hit me.

Or run away.

I reach for the tap. Instead of turning it off, I turn it cold. The water has my abs clenching, my thighs hard.

What threw me was the way she'd looked at me when I told her I saw the Memphis show. Those eyes—I still can't decide if they're brown or green, and it's starting to bug me—widened, and she'd sucked in an excited breath so big she was practically vibrating with it.

But if there's one thing I don't do on tour, it's hang out with interns.

At 2 a.m.

Alone.

By the time I step out and pull on track pants and favorite hoodie, there's a response to my message.

Lobby bar

I slip out the door and take the elevator. No one's in the lounge save the bartender and two figures in chairs hunched over a table.

But Jerry's not waiting for me because he's already playing with someone.

Haley's curled up in the opposite chair wearing purple pajama pants under a white hotel robe.

Plus slippers.

I can't remember the last time I saw a woman in slippers.

"If you do that," Jerry says, "then I'll go like this." He swipes a piece off the board, and she watches intently. He starts to reverse it, but she stops him.

"No. Take it off."

I wonder if she knows she's learning from the master. Of chess and sound engineering.

A group of people older than me come into the bar, and I flip the hood of my sweatshirt up.

Jerry's as much a legend as I am, but she doesn't pump him for information or suck up.

"I heard you got the boss's phone back."

She shrugs a shoulder without lifting her gaze from the board. "Yeah. I had to give something up to get it back, though."

I'm bristling before Jerry asks what.

"'My jacket. I mean, I can get another one, but it was my mom's. She gave it to me before she died."

My hands ball into fists, but Jerry *hmm*s over the chess board.

They play in silence for a few moves. Then he says, "If I worried you earlier, I didn't mean to."

"It's okay. I thought I did something wrong."

He makes a dismissive noise. "Being on tour is the best thing and the worst thing for a human being. It's a lonely business. There's a lot of time to spin in your head, which means we all have our...moods."

She smiles. "I get it. My roommate Serena says I have my moods too. Usually two days a month. And during midterms."

Two moves later, he has her in a checkmate.

"Thank you. For teaching me." Haley rises, and her robe slips open before she refastens the tie. "I'm going to go work on a program, but can we do this again sometime?"

"Sure. Goodnight, Miss Telfer."

"Night, Jerry."

I watch her round the corner toward the elevator before I drop into the chair she vacated.

"'Miss Telfer.' You trying to score a spot on her

dance card?" I prod as I reset the chess pieces on my side.

"I'm too old for her. So are you," he jabs with a toothy smile.

I ignore him.

Jerry wins the white pieces, and he opens with a pawn.

I match him.

"You had an appointment before we left Philly." He moves another pawn. "What'd the doctor say, Jerry?"

"I'm an old man."

"That's all?" I send my bishop along the diagonal, covering his king.

His hand trembles on the pawn as he takes mine with his. "It's Alzheimer's."

A wave of nausea washes over me and I shove it down. "This is the second doctor. You could see a third."

"No more doctors, Jax. Besides, I have help. Or didn't you notice?"

I let out a half laugh I don't feel. "I'm not worried you're going to forget to plug me in one night, Jerry. I'm worried about *you*."

"Maybe you should worry less about me and

more about you. I hear you've got another album to make."

I grimace. "Cross has been leaving messages daily. Sometimes I'm surprised he's letting me finish the tour before dragging me back in the studio."

But he can't. We agreed to a year's break before the last album I'll ever make.

"You written anything?"

If I can't talk to Jerry, I can't talk to anyone. The man's had my back since I was twenty. He might be the only one who has. "I'm not sure I have it in me. The first album was too personal. The next two…"

"There's less of you and more of them," he finishes.

I nod because he's right. The production studio takes over. Starts focus grouping and auto-tuning, and before you know it you're just one input in the marketing machine.

I take his pawn. "I've been at this a long time. I'm ready to go the hell home."

The group at the bar is laughing and drinking and oblivious to us.

I focus only on his king. He takes my bishop, sparing me a narrowed glance.

"I almost missed calling Annie on her birthday

today because I was too distracted by all of this shit." Familiar bitterness rises in the back of my throat. "Ten more stops. Then I'm done, Jerry. I'm out."

"How many albums you sold?"

My gaze works over the board between us. "Forty-six million."

"How many shows?"

"Hundred eighty-three."

"How much have you made in the last ten years?"

"Okay, now you're being rude." I lift my attention to Jerry's lined face.

"Memory serves—and I know sometimes it don't..." His face lines as he grins. "...you're the one who signed on for this shit."

"I was eighteen. Living in a one-bedroom apartment, no food and no future. Wasn't much of a choice."

Jerry glances at my bourbon. "That Bulleit?"

"You know it."

He takes it from me, sipping and making a sound of appreciation.

At least until he coughs.

"Should you be drinking that?" I ask wryly.

"I'm too old to drink bourbon. I'm too old to

walk," he replies, handing the glass back. "You ever heard of Robert Johnson?"

I shake my head.

"Bluesman from the thirties. His work was remade by Clapton. Keith Richards. Anyway. They say he was driving through Mississippi late at night when he came on a crossroads. The devil offered him the chance to turn around or take the blues in exchange for his soul. You know what he did?"

"I'm guessing he didn't turn around."

"Nope. And before he died at twenty-seven, he made some of the best damn music that's ever existed, present company included."

"What's your point?"

He grunts, his gaze never leaving the board. "You signed on the line. You chose your path, son. I'm glad you did because I wouldn't have the privilege of sitting in that box every night watching you do your work.

"Now you got another choice. You can spend your life regretting the deal you made, shutting everyone and everything out while you're at it, or"—he moves his queen down the board, and I see the checkmate too late—"you can play the blues the devil gave you."

8

HALEY

I don't bother hiding a yawn as I pull up a screen on my computer. I see how it's impossible to keep up on sleep while on tour. If I'm going to find time to work on my program without sacrificing my sleep, I need to stop playing chess and start eking out time.

"Babysitter."

Jax's voice has me glancing up from the board at the booth in the Air Canada Centre.

Today he's wearing a blue T-shirt that sets off his amber eyes and jeans over white sneakers. His hair's tucked under an Astros cap.

I don't like baseball. Or hats.

I like both on him.

"Where's Jerry?"

I nod toward the aisle. "Talking with one of the venue guys. I'm on setup."

If there's pride in my voice, it's because I am proud.

Jerry let me lead on organizing for the night ahead. Of course he'll fix all the stuff I screw up, but I get the chance to do it.

Instead of leaving, Jax moves closer, leaning his elbows on the half wall between us and running his gaze over me. I'm suddenly self-conscious in my black tank top and jeans.

"I bet you've never gotten in trouble a day in your life. At least not since the finger painting incident."

I fold my arms over my chest "Untrue. I was suspended in high school."

His eyes glint. "For what?"

"Our math teacher used to post our grades after tests. So, I started taking pictures of them. Then wrote a program correlating them with whether the students were on varsity athletic teams."

"And?"

"And—shocker—if you could kick a football, you were also a god at factoring quadratic equations." I wrinkle my nose. "But the principal seemed more concerned with my hypothesis than the findings."

"How did they find out?"

"I hacked the school's webpage and posted it there."

I dust my hands on my jeans, looking up from the board to find Jax giving me that look again. Amusement mixed with curiosity.

"You do have a little rebel in you."

Maybe he's making fun of me. Or maybe he thinks I'm cool after all.

I give myself the benefit of the doubt and a mental fist bump to boot.

"Aren't you supposed to be doing press?" I ask. "Nina will kill you if she finds you down here."

"I'm done. Media piranhas have been fed for the day, and Neen's off flirting with Brick somewhere."

I can't tell if he's joking about the last part.

"I bet they love talking about your music."

"No. They love asking if I take it up the ass." He replies so easily I'm sure I've misheard him. "Most interviewers care less about the music and more about my lifestyle." He cocks his head, a smirk on handsome face as he leans in. "In case you're curious, I told them only from my label."

I can't believe how supremely comfortable he is with *everything*. As if he could strip naked right here and walk up on that stage wearing nothing but the smirk and be completely self-possessed.

After last night, I'd promised to take Lita's advice and keep things strictly business. Because I lost a night's sleep imagining him with those women. I need to stay focused on my work.

But I didn't promise I wouldn't talk to him.

"I want to talk about music," I blurt.

He recovers from the flicker of surprise almost immediately, spreading his hands. "Ask away."

"Last night, you were going to tell me about seeing Leonard Cohen."

"So I was."

He does.

I hang on every word as he describes the concert, and the way he talks about it, I can picture myself there.

Then we go through our favorite concerts of all time, trading stories. I can't believe how many shows he's been to.

"I would've thought you'd never get to any shows."

"On tour it's hard," Jax admits. "But sometimes it's all that keeps you sane."

An alert beeps on my phone, reminding me of my task. "Shit. I need to get this finished."

With a moment's hesitation, he rounds the half wall and comes to stand next to me. He takes one look at the setup I'm doing and reaches for the board, flicking switches like he's playing an arcade game.

My jaw drops. "What are you doing?"

"Array configuration's different here than Pittsburgh." He bends over, checking a connection under the board before straightening. All of his focus is on the dials as his hands move over them. "You need to accommodate for that in the mix."

He realizes I've gone still, and mute, and stops, sighing. "The array's the speakers stacked by the stage—"

"I know what an array is," I mumble.

That's not the problem.

The problem is that Jax Jamieson knows how to do my job.

He just got fifty per cent hotter. Which is a statistical impossibility, because the man's already on par with the sun.

Stay professional. He's basically your boss.

Who's eight years older and has a sleeve of tattoos

and who you have a poster of in your room like you're twelve instead of twenty.

He finishes what he was doing, then shifts a hip against the board as he turns to face me.

"So, the app you built," he says casually, cutting into my daydreams. "It tells you how to mix better songs."

Get a grip. I shake myself. "Um. In theory."

"To make money."

"Sort of. But also for science." I click into competent mode and out of "drooling on the floor" mode. "It tells us things about our brains and how we relate to music. Some people would say that's even more interesting."

"People like you."

"Well. Yeah."

"How does it decide what's 'good'?"

"It's based on a database of hit songs from the last fifty years. Including yours."

"Mine?" He cocks his head. "How many of them."

"All of them," I confess. "I couldn't decide what to leave off. 'Redline' has this guitar hook that won't quit. 'Inside' is this acoustic exploration that guts you, then resolves right when you'd swear it won't." I swallow, feeling hot all of a sudden.

Maybe it's because his stare has intensified or because it feels like I'm spilling my guts. "In case no one's told you, you're kind of a genius," I finish.

That hangs between us for a good five seconds, and I'm cursing myself for going too fangirl.

"People probably tell you that every day. I can stop."

His jaw works, but there's a glint of something in his eyes.

"Jax! You want in on sound check?" someone calls from the stage.

He stares at me a second longer before pulling something from his pocket and setting it on the board.

Then Jax jogs up to the front and plugs in his guitar. He grabs a stool and pulls it up to the mic.

He starts to play, and I glance down to realize he's left me his phone.

Again.

Like the last three shows.

What did he do with it before this?

Is it weird that I don't really care?

I lift the phone in my hand, turning it over. It's warm from his pocket. The smooth surface is marred by scratches, and I wonder how they got there.

"Strange." I turn to find Jerry at my back, setting his bag gently down on the chair.

"What's that?" I stare at the board, wondering which of my settings I've gotten wrong.

"He hasn't done sound check in weeks."

My gaze follows Jerry's toward the stage.

And now I'm thinking dirty thoughts about a rock star.

It should be innocent, but it's not. Not when I know he has a girlfriend. Not when I'm here to do a job.

The fact that I have zero chance with him doesn't matter in the slightest. It's the principle of it.

The phone burns a hole in my pocket through the final sound check. After, Jax vanishes from stage to get ready.

The rise of the curtain. The opening act. The main event.

The next hours fly by working with Jerry. He's so competent, and he always knows what to do.

Except at one point he stops, staring at the board.

"What is it?" I ask him.

"I don't…"

I've noticed that before, what's possibly the

reason Cross assigned me here. Jerry has lapses. He'll remember everything about the venue, the acoustics, the tech, but he'll forget people he's supposed to meet or what time he's supposed to be on-site.

I open my notes from earlier, check, and point at the setting he'd told me about. "Is it this one?"

He nods, and we finish the show.

Eight encores.

I've never seen a band play eight encores, but Jax, Brick, Kyle, and Mace do it as if it's the last night of their lives.

At the ninth encore, my pocket buzzes.

I don't want to look at it. Don't want to be pulled out of this.

But when it buzzes again with a text from Annie, I do.

Call me back
Please
Something bad happened

Fear streaks down my spine as I lean over Jerry. "I have to go."

I cut through the halls, finding my way to backstage and flashing my pass to get through. The ninth encore is the last, and Jax comes off the stage, the building nearly falling down from the roar of the crowd. Sweat's running down his forehead as he chugs water next to the stage.

His gaze lands on me.

"It's Annie," I pant. "Something's wrong."

His body goes stiff as if he's been shot. Then he grabs the phone from my hand and stalks toward the dressing rooms.

I'm not sure if I'm supposed to follow him, but I can't not.

"Annie. What is it, baby?" I hear him say.

My chest tightens. I realize I've followed him right into his dressing room, but I can't leave. I'm rooted to the spot.

He listens, and I'm desperate to know what's happening, but I can't hear the voice on the other end.

After a moment, though, Jax's shoulders slump. "Division? Yeah, that sucks. Okay. It's late. I'll call you in the morning." I start to duck out, but he crooks a finger, telling me to stay. "We'll do all the math you want."

When Jax hangs up, he crosses to the old-fashioned wooden dressing table at the far end and reaches for a towel to wipe his face. He braces his hands on the wood, still breathing heavily from the show as he meets my gaze in the mirror. "She lives for social studies, but math is the devil. Ten-year-olds' drama."

"Ten years old?" I'm still struggling to catch up with the wry twist in his mouth.

"Annie's my niece."

I drop onto the couch, the fake leather smooth on my bare shoulders as my eyes fall closed.

"Who'd you think she was?" There's curiosity in his tone, and an odd edge.

"I don't know. You have pictures of a woman in your bus. Your arm's around her."

He hesitates barely a second. "My little sister, Grace."

I don't normally get wrapped up in other people's lives, but I couldn't have predicted the cascade of emotions that follows. It's like dominos, shock chasing understanding chasing anticipation chasing hope, until one crashes into the next and leaves me a bundle of humming nerves.

Part of me's filled with dread and the rest wants to jump for joy.

The fact that you're alone with Jax Jamieson in his dressing room and he's single changes nothing.

He's not a sex symbol. He's an artist, a business person, a...

My rambling thought train comes to a screeching halt when I blink my eyes open. A sensory spectacle on the other side of the room accosts me in slow motion.

Jax Jamieson is stripping his shirt over his head. His back muscles ripple, and my eyes trace the tattoos over his arm, across his shoulder, to where they end midway down his back.

This is so much more than the poster. It's surround sound Dolby hotness, and as he turns, showing off equally sexy chest, all I can think about is what it would be like to trace those lines with—

"You thought I had a girlfriend. And that bothered you." He totally caught me staring.

My lips move, but nothing comes out. "Yes," I manage finally. "Because you go to that room to party. Not for any other reason."

He stares me down like he can see every dirty thought in my twisted head. "You don't need to save my soul, Hales." The nickname sends prickles through me. "But I like that you want to."

I have a long moment to soak in the effect of his gorgeous body from under my half-lowered lashes before he reaches for a T-shirt. Then drags a black hoodie over that.

I bet you wouldn't take a bath after he touched you. The random thought invades my brain.

He crosses to the couch, and when his gaze drops to my bare arms, any trace of a smirk vanishes. "You're shivering."

"It's fine."

"Where's your jacket."

I swallow. "I lost it."

And holy shit, it must be my birthday because he's reaching for the hem of his shirt again.

Scratch that. His sweatshirt.

He strips it over his head in a way that tugs his T-shirt up a few tantalizing inches before dropping it down again.

He holds it out to me.

"You're loaning me your sweatshirt?"

"Keep it."

"Oh. I couldn't."

"You have a problem with accepting help, don't you?"

My brows pull together. "No! I mean… only if I haven't earned it. I don't like people feeling sorry for me."

Just when I'm about to reach for it, he seems to reconsider. Before I can protest, he grabs a sharpie off a table across the room and scrawls something on the fabric. I lift my hands fast enough to catch the shirt he tosses at my head. "There. Now it's personalized. You can't give it back."

My fingers dig into the soft fabric.

"Thank you." I want to tell him I love it. Instead, I hold the sweater up by the shoulders. "I can't see what you wrote."

"Just as well." I'm totally imagining the teasing note in his voice as he drops onto the couch next to me.

The shirt smells like laundry soap and him, and until he smirks, I don't realize I'm smelling it.

Shit.

I don't know why I'm still here, or why he is, but I'm afraid to change a thing.

"Why do people feel sorry for you."

I blow out a breath. "My mom died last year. In a car accident. She'd come home from a work trip to take me to a concert for my birthday. On the way back, it was raining. She had to hit her brakes to stop from running into a car in front of her. The eighteen wheeler behind her couldn't stop in time."

His nostrils flare. "Your dad?"

I shake my head. "He's never been in my life. I don't know who he is."

The way his mouth twists at the corner is dark. "Hope it was a good concert."

Death makes most people squirm. His response should make me angry, or indignant.

It's satisfying somehow because I know he's not laughing at my mom or the terrible thing that happened to her.

He's laughing at life. If there's one thing I've learned, it's that if you can't laugh at life's coincidences—the good things and the bad things and the horrible ones—you might as well be dead.

"It was," I say finally.

"Whose?"

"Yours."

I'm used to seeing shock on people's faces when they hear what happened, but Jax recovers quickly.

"Your mom died coming back from my concert and now you're on my tour. That's twisted." I half expect him to walk out but he just studies me. "Is this some kind of retribution thing?"

"No. Not even a little." I shift forward, bringing our faces close enough I can see the dark flecks in his gold eyes.

"See, I put on your music—*Inside* actually— and played it on repeat for weeks. My friend Serena says she doesn't know how I was so strong. The thing is I wasn't. You were. You were there for me, and you didn't even know it."

I take a breath because now that I've started, I can't seem to stop.

"That's what made me start building this program. It's also my biggest problem. Computers can analyze pitch and frequency and levels and what's pleasing to the human ear. Machine learning algorithms can predict hits on the basis of what's come before. But what none of it can do is tell you what kind of person creates those songs. What they're thinking, feeling, when they do.

"I want to know that," I say, breathless. "I want to know *you*."

Silence stretches between us. Except it's not really. I can hear sounds of metal on metal in the hallway. Of footsteps.

Neither of us looks toward the door.

Jax looks like he's turning something over in his mind. He smells like sandalwood and sweat. Like he came back from battle.

"I wrote 'Inside' when I thought I was going to die. When I was out of control. I don't play it, I don't even let anyone cover it, because it takes me back there."

I swallow the sudden thickness in my throat. "I heard about your parents. I never heard you had a sister."

"I don't like paparazzi harassing what family I have left. I left Dallas to make a better life for my family. But my little sister got knocked around by this guy while I was recording. She married him when I was on tour. Now they're raising Annie together. If I'd been there instead of here, this wouldn't have happened."

My chest squeezes, hard. I see why he carries so much around with him, but there's something wrong about what he's saying.

"How do you know it wouldn't have happened if you were there?"

His jaw tightens. "I just do. It's why I count down every show in this damned tour until I can go home and make up for all of it."

Jax looks as if he's going to say something, but his intake of breath has me looking down.

"Jax, your fingers are bleeding." I frown, resisting the urge to grab his hands to take a better look. "I used to bite my nails."

He scoffs. "From playing guitar." But he holds my gaze for a beat. Two. "How'd you stop?"

"I glued peanuts on them."

His brows shoot up into his hairline. "Holy shit, really?"

"No, not really."

Laughter starts somewhere deep inside him, warm and full and incredulous.

And like that, the whole world is me and him, the dimple in his cheek I've somehow never noticed, the light in his eyes as our bodies rock.

"Well?" Jax asks finally, his gaze dropping to the sweatshirt clutched in my hands. "You gonna put it on or just cuddle?"

The fabric bunches in my fingers. I don't take my gaze from his as I shift on the couch, tugging his sweatshirt over my head.

I didn't expect it to be warm and comforting, but more than that...

God it smells like him. It's all fabric softener

and man, and if fame had a scent I know it would be this.

I shove the hood back, resisting the temptation to fix my hair.

"There," he says, a hint of satisfaction in his voice as his amber eyes darken.

"What?"

"It's like I'm touching you everywhere."

Words like "boss" and "distance" and "older" fall away because they can't compete with that.

When the biggest rock star on the planet says "I'm touching you everywhere" because you put on his hoodie, it's the biggest tease in the world.

But Jax looks completely relaxed when he shoves at the hair falling over his forehead, sliding a tattooed arm along the back of the couch. Curiosity edges into his expression. "So the whole hating it when strangers touch you thing... that's only strangers, right? It doesn't stop you from doing other stuff."

"What kind of other stuff." My ears are ringing.

He lifts a brow. "Like sex."

I stare him down but the only thing in his expression is concern. It's as if he appointed himself my personal therapist without telling me, or asking permission.

"Right," I manage. "Yeah, I have sex. But I don't like to drag it out. You know. It's better if it's fast."

Dark brows draw together on his face as if maybe I'm speaking another language. "Shit," he says finally. "That's a damned crime, Hales, because the best sex?" Jax's eyes glint as he stretches out his legs, dragging my gaze down his hard, perfect body without permission. "The best sex is *slow*."

I think I stop breathing when he says it.

He looks as if he's not aware of the effect he's having. I think he likes having someone to talk to who's not interested in him.

If only that were true, I think as I sneak a look at him from under my lashes.

The first time I met him, I was beyond intimidated.

When he's like this, he doesn't seem older or different or scary.

Jax Jamieson is timeless.

He's perfect.

The door opens, and Mace sticks his head in. "Jax, Nina's asking if you can do an appearance tomorrow at…"

He trails off as he sees us. "Am I interrupting?"

"No." He hesitates, and for a second, I want

him to say yes. Yes, you're interrupting. Please go away and come back in an hour.

Or never.

"Let's get out of here." Jax shifts out from under me and follows his bandmate out the door.

I stare after him.

Until this moment, I wasn't sure why I'm on this tour.

Jax Jamieson has saved me more times than I can count.

Maybe it's my turn to save him.

Haley: I figured out what you wrote on the sweatshirt.

Jax: ??

Haley: Good luck wearing this when it's ninety degrees.

Jax: AC broke on ur bus?

Haley: No, but Lita likes to sit on top of it when she's managing her fantasy baseball team.

Haley: She says a cool ass makes for a cooler head and she makes better trades this way.

Jax: tell hr she can't have altuve

Haley: She gave you the finger. Who's Altuve?

Jax: ask her typing 2 hrd

Haley: You could always get a real phone.

Jax: blsphemy

Haley: Seriously. Save those million-dollar
fingers for something worthwhile.

Haley: Like playing guitar. Or building LEGO.

Jax: no point

Jax: mace is 2 proud 2 let me hlp ;)

———————

Haley,

Good to hear you're enjoying the summer. You're only young once.

I've uploaded some comments in the attached files. The program needs a lot of work before we can submit it to Spark, but I know you can get it there.

Talk soon,

Chris

———

By Kansas City, we're falling into a routine.

Five shows in and not only can I hold a flip phone, I can work the soundboard. Not quite by myself because Jerry's still the master. But I'm getting better. I like the combination of digital and analog.

I sneak out a bit of time to work on my program. Mostly at night after the shows because it helps me transition to sleeping. I've built in ideas Jax has shared with me.

Though I'm not about to admit it because his

ego would blow up.

Some nights I play with Jerry. His mind's not great, but he's amazing at chess, and I've learned he's the most patient teacher.

I've also learned Jax looks after him. He drops by the sound booth before every gig, usually with the excuse to check on something. But they end up talking and joking for a few minutes, sometimes half an hour. That much time might not seem like a lot, but I'm realizing that when you're headlining a production like this one? It's a lifetime.

This morning should feel like every other morning. The surroundings are the same. But since Toronto, I've been edgy.

I spend a lot of time thinking about Jax.

We all do because it's his tour.

I'm guessing the others don't sniff his hoodie and wear it to bed.

Miss placing a coffee order because they're picturing his body. Or that smirk.

It's reasonable that I'm a little distracted since finding out that the voice in the phone I'd assumed was his girlfriend is actually in third grade.

Sue me for being happy. I'm never touching Jax and he's never touching me.

Still.

I feel better about the times my gaze lingers on him, knowing there's not someone out there who's earned the right.

Serena calls me right after lunch.

"How're you getting off?"

"Huh?"

"I said how are you getting on?"

"Oh." We've stopped at a diner where I wolfed down a sandwich. Now, I'm sneaking a few moments of privacy behind the bus. "It's weird being around people 24/7."

"I thought you had your own room?"

"I do. But even then..." I struggle to explain it. "It's like you can't forget the whole crew is sleeping a few steps away."

"Creepy." I laugh. "The tuition bill arrived."

The smile fades. "When's it due?"

"August."

I curse. "I haven't gotten a paycheck yet. That competition better work out. I have another two weeks before the deadline. If we win..."

"You're rolling in cash."

"At least I'm rolling in enough to pay for next semester."

"Please tell me you're not spending every

waking moment working on that computer program."

"Carter sent me a bunch of tweaks to work on. Basically, I need different versions of the same track, so I'm going through these databases to find—"

"Whoa." I stop. "When are you going to lift your head from Carter's ass and look around?"

"I am looking around. And then I realize I'm on a rock tour, and it's insane, and I put my head down again."

I've listened to everyone I can to learn the business. Production crew members setting up. Nina rattling off orders like a Smurfette drill sergeant. To Jax, whether he's fine-tuning an arrangement with the band or giving feedback to the lighting director or reviewing the promotion schedule with Nina.

Something I've learned in between the 'actual' work is that not only does Jax look after Jerry, he looks after everyone.

He buys every meal for every crew member when we're traveling. Ensures there's a massage therapist, physiotherapist, or doctor on site the moment anyone groans, cracks, or coughs.

"The universe is change. Our life is what our thoughts make of it."

Serena's voice brings me back and I blink at the side of the bus. "Did you just quote Marcus Aurelius?"

"You think I don't remember anything from that first-year philosophy course we took together?"

"You're kind of awesome. So, how's Declan? Or Nolan?"

"Oh, I'm so past that. But there's this guy, Tristan..."

I grin as she tells me all about him.

"How's your man quest?"

"No quest. And no men." I hesitate. "But I have seen more of Jax than I expected. He...tolerates me."

"Sounds hot," she says dryly.

I chew my lip, looking around to make sure I'm alone in the parking lot. "More like we're... friend-ly." I realize as I say it that it's true. "He talks to me about all kinds of things, and I think he trusts me." I don't want to admit that we text each other, because that feels personal. Serena making up crazy sex ideas is one thing, but this is too close to real and I hate that she'd try to read something into this.

I glance up as the crew starts to file out of the restaurant. "I gotta go. Thanks for calling."

"What?! You can't leave."

"Serena, I have to—"

"Ugh, fine. And Haley? Don't worry about where you came from. Think about where you are right now. Which is the Riot Act tour."

We hang up, and an hour later I'm sitting on our bus, heading to the next town. Most of the crew is playing cards in the back when Jerry drops onto the seat, and I realize there's a photo album in his hands.

"Oh, here we go," Lita comments from the opposite couch, where she's reviewing what I've learned are stats on her iPad.

"Shush," Jerry scorns.

I look between them, mystified.

"It's a rite of passage," she clarifies. "Tour rule number seventy-two: thou shalt be subjected to the History of Music According to Jerry."

But as the old man flips through the pages, it's not boring.

It's fascinating.

There are more famous faces than I can count.

Moments captured on film, painstakingly tucked into sheets.

"You made all this yourself?"

"Sure did." His leathered fingers turn the pages.

We stop on a picture of Jerry drinking beer next to... God, is that Prince?

"You were badass."

"Started out as a stagehand. But I always loved sound. Took me five years before they'd let me near it."

He turns some more pages.

"That's..."

"CEO himself." Cross is way younger in the picture. "First few years after he founded Wicked. Didn't own a suit yet."

"It looks like a party." My gaze scans the other people in the picture. Rests on one.

"See? That haircut is worth blackmailing over."

"It's not the haircut. Do you know that woman?"

"No. Can't say's I do. Do you?"

I frown. "Can I grab a copy of this?"

"Don't show anyone." He winks. "He doesn't go anywhere without a suit anymore."

I lift my phone and snap a picture.

When I close out of the photo app, I see a message from Carter. I bite my cheek and reach for my laptop.

"What's that?" Jerry asks.

"Just working on an app I built for this competition."

His eyes light up. "A what?"

I get out of the terminal mode and switch into the graphics-laden interface that's more user-friendly. "So you import a track, then choose from one of these settings..."

His hand points to one of the three buttons on the screen.

"Yeah. Exactly."

The app's not perfect yet, but what strikes me is that Jerry immediately grasps how to use it.

Probably because the interface is clean and straightforward. I even modeled part of it after an analog soundboard, though it was more for whimsy than any legit reason.

Which gives me an idea.

Lita and her bassist are on the couch up front with

me when I close my computer two hours later. "What are you guys working on?"

"New song. After this tour wraps, we're going out on our own. I have a friend who's set up some gigs in Nashville for us. Small venues. Different than playing arenas, but it'll be our show. Our way."

I shift back into the seat. It's my day off, and I'm determined to think about something that's not Jax for ten seconds. "So, what are you guys doing in KC?"

She fires off a message on her phone, then holds up a finger and grins at the response. "Kyle's in."

My brows shoot up. "Kyle's in on what?"

Lita explains, and I shift in my seat, playing with my phone. Serena's words echo in my head.

"Can I come with you?"

That's how five hours later, I'm no longer a college-student-turned-sound-tech-assistant. I'm watching Lita's band in a little bar in Kansas City, drinking bourbon she bought for me that she swears will change my life.

I don't know about life-changing, but it's sweet and spicy and has all my internal organs on notice.

Kyle's on drums, looking as happy as when he

plays a stadium. Lita's swinging her hips as she sings, crooning into the mic.

The crowd's barely thirty people, but they're into it. It's thrilling—or maybe that's the bourbon again—until she steps off stage between songs and motions me up. "Come on. I know you can sing. I've heard you on the bus."

I stumble after her, a little slow thanks to the spirits. "I don't know your songs well enough."

We stop in front of Kyle, and she says, "What do you know well enough?"

I look around the stage. Whether it's the drinks or Serena's voice in my head, an idea takes over my mind.

I bite my lip before I say the word.

Kyle shifts back on his stool.

But Lita's beaming. "It's a song, Kyle, not a cursed monkey paw. Take the mic, Haley."

I step up to it. The chords start, and I lose myself in the song.

My favorite song.

It starts somewhere deep in me, uncurling like a flower.

The song that's always gotten me through the moments I don't feel independent, ready, or capable.

The times I wish my mom were still here.

The times I wonder who my father is.

The times I feel like something's wrong with me.

My eyes fall shut, and I sing.

I lose track of time.

I don't care about the crowd, about anything.

When my eyes open, they find one person in particular.

A guy wearing a long-sleeve black T-shirt and an Astros cap.

My heart is in my throat as he spins and stalks out the door.

10

"The National Museum of Toys and Miniatures," Mace reads off his iPad.

"You want to spend our first day off in weeks looking at Barbies?" Kyle snorts.

"Says the asshole who shaved his head last year to support the preservation of finger monkey habitat."

"They're called pygmy marmosets," Kyle tosses back.

"You coming, Jax?" Mace asks, a look of neediness on his face.

My criteria are usually where can I get time outside and where won't I be recognized. I'm guessing the toy museum is as good a place as any to go incognito.

So I trail Mace around the museum as he pops his gum and points stuff out.

"What's eating you? Is it Grace and Annie?" Mace asks as we stop next to a glass case of wooden Disney toys from the 1930s. The paint on Mickey's face is curling.

He's the most perceptive person I know. Maybe that's why he struggled so much with drugs. Because he sees things, feels things. Needs to numb out the world.

I shrug. "They used to come at least three times on a tour. In between, we'd talk almost every day. Now, I've been trying to get Grace to come for three months. Nothing."

I brush past him, and we make our way through the last hall.

We go out for dinner, finding a patio to enjoy the summer weather. My ball cap is jammed down, sunglasses on, and even though our waitress looks a little too long, if she knows something, she doesn't say.

"Once this tour's done, we got another studio album to record."

I bite into my hamburger, then wash it down with beer. "I know."

"You really have nothing?"

I pull a sheet of paper from my pocket and hold it out to him.

"You need to get a phone from this century so you can write in Notes like a grownup," he mumbles, spilling ketchup in his lap.

"Says the guy who puts ketchup on his calamari."

"You can put ketchup on anything."

But I wait as he reads the notes I've been making. Some are lyrics. Some are chords, which will get translated into vibrations, sounds, in his mind as easily as they do in mine.

"What do you think?" I ask.

"I think everything you've written since 'Midnight Mass' gets a little further from who you are."

"I'm not that kid anymore."

"This"—he holds up the paper—"isn't who you are either. At least 'Midnight Mass' was the most honest shit you ever wrote."

I take back the sheet. "You ever write?"

He shrugs. "Sure. Back before you picked me up. In the dark ages." He grins.

"You ever think about whether you're writing to affect people or just get it out? And when you do, where do you start? The music or the words."

"Never thought about it."

"It used to come to me like a storm. The riff. Then when it got too much, it'd rip through me. By the time I finished, the words were there." I turn it over in my head. "Maybe that's the problem."

He studies me, a look of realization dawning. "Or the problem is you're overthinking it. This is about Haley, isn't it? I should've known there was something going on when I walked in on you. She was wearing your hoodie, man."

It's such a high school thing to say, but I don't have a good explanation except she pulled me in by being genuinely interested in my ideas. The questions she ask challenge me in a real way, unlike the ones I've been fielding for years.

"She's twenty."

"It's legal."

"It's not like that."

"She's pretty."

I swallow the laugh. "So are a lot of women."

"And I can't remember the last time you looked at any of 'em." He shifts back in his chair. "Jax. You signed up to be a musician, not a monk. You can't hold one mistake against yourself for a lifetime."

"Haley's not that kind of girl."

"Not the kind you fuck or the kind you walk away from?"

I turn it over. "Either."

For starters, Cross has rules about fraternization on tour, and they're my rules too.

Plus, she's too young for me. For anyone here. Haley's off-limits on that basis alone.

Even if she wasn't, there's no way I could tug her down the hall and into my room.

She'd barely let me touch her hand.

Not to mention pin her up against the wall with my hips to fit her slow curves to my body.

If I lowered my mouth to hers, those big brown eyes would be as big as satellites.

If I kissed her, pressed the seam of her full lips with my tongue until she opened...

She'd probably bite me.

"You okay?"

I blink up at Mace, shaking off the daydream. "Yeah."

Mace pops the last of his fried octopus into his mouth, making a noise low in his throat. "You remember that first tour?" he asks.

I push Haley from my mind. "We were fucking idiots."

He grunts his agreement, draining the rest of his beer. "Best time of my life."

I don't remind him that what followed was him falling down the rabbit hole.

I knew his using had gotten out of hand before our second tour. But that was when we had our moment, when I told him he had to get clean or I'd cut him out. He begged me to reconsider. But I held firm in the face of my best friend, needle marks in his arm and his heart rate exploding.

We spend the next hour drinking beer and reminiscing about the good times. It's dark when Mace glances at his phone, snorting. He holds it up.

"What the hell is that?" I ask.

"The bar Kyle's at."

"Wanna go see if he's chained himself to the bar in defense of single-origin rye?"

"Nah, man." He sticks the phone away. "I'm going back to the hotel."

I consider it, then I decide I'm not ready to go back just yet.

Our car drops him off first, and my eyes fall closed as my head drops back against the seat. Instead of thinking about Annie or Grace or the next seven tour stops, I think about Haley.

Maybe she is in my head.

Yeah, she's young. But she acts more mature

than Mace most of the time.

When a smart woman tells you she wants to *know* you, she wants to keep your secrets and hear your problems?

It's damn hard to resist.

I know Jerry relies on her help, and she's like a sponge. Some interns have this sense of entitlement. They try to avoid the shit jobs.

Haley'll take on anything, so long as you tell her what it's about.

I respect the hell out of that. Especially since I know what her life's been like the last year.

I've been through it too.

The car pulls up at the bar, and I shake off the thoughts as I step out and start toward the open door.

The chords drifting from inside clamp down on my heart.

The closer I get to the entrance, the more my steps slow.

I can't go in, but neither can I stop. The bouncer glances at my face just long enough to see I'm of age, then he holds the door for me.

The words reach my ears as I step inside.

"All the primary colors

Burn my eyes

I'm black and white

Encased in lies

And everything blurs in between

I'm lighter fluid and gasoline

Inside"

She's there, on the stage with Lita and Kyle. Her jeans are ripped at the knees. Her tank top leaves miles of skin on display under the blue stage lights.

Not that she notices, because her eyes are closed as she sings my song in a voice as clear as a bell.

My fucking song.

As if she can feel me, her eyes open.

Long-buried hopelessness clashes with new betrayal, like waves from opposing tides.

I'm jerked back to a time when I was all help-lessness, no control. I hate that she can make me feel this way.

Without a word, I spin and shove out the doors.

I need a car. But I can't wait that long to stab a number on my phone.

It's my turn to get voicemail.

"Cross. Take her back. I don't know why you sent her, but you're going to take her the fuck back."

11

HALEY

"My name is Jax Jamieson. I'm eighteen years old."

The camera jerks like he knocked it as he picks up his guitar.

I notice, but like the people responsible for the last eighty million online video views, I don't care.

I watch the boy in the dark, his fingers plucking the guitar, picking up speed. Hear his voice that begins over the top, playing between the notes of the strings. Soaking into them like rain into the hungry ground.

Which version hits me harder? The one almost my age, desperate and raw, or the one ten years later? The one who's seen everything, built the armor—and cynicism—that comes with being in the spotlight?

"Mace orders lobster at every diner. It's going to bite him in the ass one day."

I snap the laptop closed as Lita shifts into the booth next to me. I pop out my earbuds and wrap the cord before setting them on my computer.

I glance a few booths down at where Jax, Kyle, Brick, and Mace are going over details for tonight with Nina. Kyle's half listening, simultaneously engaged in a discussion with the waitress about what looks like the plastic straws. Mace enthusiastically devours whatever's on his plate. Brick throws a french fry at Nina as if he's ten years old and learning to flirt. She turns her head, the picture of the equanimity preached in the books she reads in the stolen moments between tour stops. The potato bounces off her blue ponytail and falls into the booth.

Jax stares out the window, one arm slung over the back of the booth, as though he's contemplating the universe.

"You're in the doghouse." Lita's grin fades as she looks between Jax and me.

I snap out of it, shaking my head. "It's a misunderstanding."

Texas is the kind of hot that makes you wonder what you did to deserve it. I swipe at a chunk of hair that's fallen out of my ponytail and stuck to my forehead.

Jax hasn't texted me since he walked out of the bar. My two messages to him have gone unanswered.

He's acting as though I betrayed him by playing his song. I spent the entire night staring at the ceiling of my hotel room and feeling as though I'd violated some code.

"Well, you were great. Really. Check this out." She pops up a video of my performance and hands me earbuds. "To be safe."

It's weird to see myself on stage, but it's pretty good. I pick at my salad as I watch and listen.

"It's okay," I say, pulling out the headphones.

"You're good, new girl. I see you working on that program. I've watched a lot of new people on tour. You're like the lifers. You keep going back for more. What're you doing after?"

"Back to Philly. Finish up my project. Then senior year starts in September."

"Until then?"

I shrug.

"We're going to Nashville. Playing honky-tonks for a few months. You should come with. We'd have fun together."

"I need to make some money."

"Can you bartend? A friend owns one of the honky-tonks. There's always a wait list to serve, but I could put in a good word. You'd get killer tips."

My eyebrows rise.

The idea's crazy, but it pulls at my mind as I shift out of the booth and start toward the counter. The coffee's actually pretty good, and—

I squeak as I collide with a wall emerging from the bathroom.

I know it's him before I look up into those eyes. "Sorry. I didn't see you."

He bends to grab his wallet. He's wearing the Astros hat again, and under that, his jaw works.

"Can I help y'all?"

We both turn toward the waitress at the counter.

"Yeah. Can I get a coffee to go?" I ask.

"And I'm going to pick up the bill," Jax mutters.

The waitress smiles. "Which bill?"

"All of them."

"No," I interrupt. "I'll pay for mine."

"I said I'll take them all," Jax says, his voice hardening.

"And I said thank you but no."

Jax drops a black card on the counter, and that, apparently, is the end of the discussion.

The waitress grabs the card and hits a few buttons on the register. "Shoot. Out of paper. One sec."

She retreats to a back room, and I'm stuck standing next to him.

It's hard to remind myself he's irrational when he's doing such a seriously decent thing. "Jax. About last night—"

"Don't." The syllable is flat against the back-drop of laughter and music in the diner. "And don't do that female thing where you make this a thing. This isn't a thing."

"Yeah, arguing in front of everyone makes it look like it's not a thing."

His exhale sounds like a punishment.

"Jax. I sang your song because I love it."

"I told you what it meant to me."

"So you don't want anyone to play it ever because it hurts you? Because you were out of control? Newsflash. We all have moments like that, Jax. Not all of them have eighty million witnesses, that's all. Maybe your pain can help someone else cope with theirs."

The waitress returns and runs Jax's card. "Wow,

I thought you looked familiar. Can I get an autograph?"

"On the bill or for you?" The grin he flashes has the waitress blinking at him.

"Both, I guess."

The reversal shouldn't hurt me, but it does. His easy smile for the waitress digs into my side like a piece of glass I can't get out. It's all I can do to wait for my coffee.

Jax signs something for her then strides out the door.

"He's something else, isn't he?" she murmurs as she hands me my cup.

"Yeah. He is."

I glance at the floor. There's a scrap of paper on it, and I think it's his receipt until I unfold it.

12

When we roll into Dallas, I go straight to my hotel to clean up and get ready for interviews.

I swipe my key by the door and crank the handle. It takes me a minute to notice the man sitting in the armchair in the corner, one ankle crossed over the knee of his suit.

"What are you doing here?"

"Unlike you, I check my voicemails." Cross sounds amused.

I stalk toward the bathroom, stripping off my shirt, feeling Cross's presence behind me.

Without looking at him, I kick off my shoes. Yank off my socks. The marble shower is cold under my feet. I crank the water to cold, and it rains on my chest, making the hairs on my neck stand up.

"You know, when I found you, you were living on mac and cheese and trying to keep your sister away from child services. Your mother was in jail. Your father dead. You couldn't keep a job. I saved you."

Cross's gaze never moves from mine as the spray rains down on my face, my chest, my thighs.

"Now apparently I'm here to save you again." He studies me. "You really hate her so much you'd call me to fix it? Is she bad at her job? Does she disrupt the rest of the crew? Because Jerry has had nothing but glowing comments both times I asked him."

Discomfort works through me because it's a resounding no to all of those. "She's just there. Asking things she shouldn't ask. Doing things she shouldn't do."

Making me feel things I have no desire to feel. Ever again.

Cross doesn't press me. "Well, I want something too. Extend the tour. Two months."

Icy cold steals my breath, making my abs flex involuntarily. "And you'll take Haley back."

"No. Two months and you'll keep her."

I turn, letting the water run down my back as I look at him. Somehow with him, I feel as though I'm eighteen again. "Why did you even send her here. To piss me off?"

I turn off the shower and step out, reaching for a towel.

"You know what it's like to learn there's someone in your life you didn't expect. Someone you can help," he says.

"You're not helping me." I wrap the towel around my waist, not bothering to dry my hair.

"I'm helping her."

Haley's face flashes in my mind, and it confuses the hell out of me why he dragged her into this. "Some college intern? An orphan, no less. Can't see why you'd bother. She's not like me—you can't make money out of her."

"She's not an orphan."

My heartbeat slows. I'm standing in the middle of the floor, dripping wet, and I can't move. He shakes his head, and the awful pieces click into place.

"Does she...?"

"She doesn't know. For a time, I didn't either. I only recently learned about her mother's death." He tugs at the collar of his shirt. The only indication he's uncomfortable. "She needed a job. What kind of father would I be to leave her out?"

My throat works, and in that moment, I hate her and feel for her at the same time.

The woman I can't get out of my head came from the man I've spent the last decade trying to leave behind.

Now I can see it in his face, in hers. The resemblance.

"Now, let's talk about how things will play out. If you care at all about her, you won't tell her and you won't ask her to leave. I will tell her in my own time."

"You want me to lie to her."

"I want time," he corrects. "You get time too. Another two months of tour stops."

The tile is cool under my feet as I pass him, crossing onto the red carpet of the living area. "And if I say no?"

"Maybe I'll decide that trust fund I've put together for Haley is better invested elsewhere."

There's his play. I should have known he'd have one. "You want me to choose between my family and yours."

"I want you to make a small concession in your life to open up a world of possibility in hers."

I can say I hate Haley. That I don't give a shit what happens to her.

But it's a lie.

I know what it's like to be where she's been, and the way she handles it, the grace, the optimism... I wish I'd been that mature at twenty.

"I won't give up everything for someone I barely know. Someone who's your responsibility, not mine."

With a half smile, Cross strides toward the door, adjusting his cuffs.

"Think it over. You have one week to decide."

13

HALEY

ho're the passes for?" I ask Nina, glancing at the table backstage by security.

"Jax has visitors tonight."

"Annie and Grace are coming?" My heart lifts.

I wish he'd told me, but we haven't spoken since yesterday in the diner.

I should be pissed at him. He's being a baby.

But the piece of paper burns a hole in my pocket.

The words on it are evidence that he's trying. That even if he doesn't want anyone to know, he hasn't given up. He's still trying to create.

A cord wrapped around each arm, I start past the band's dressing room on my way to meet Jerry at the soundboard.

The silence is strange, and I stick my head in. Every face in the room looks at me.

Or rather they look at Nina, who passes me, her tablet in hand.

It's not unusual for Jax to be late. But someone else is missing.

"Where's Mace?" she asks.

A groan from the corner of the room answers her question. The bassist is curled up on a bean bag chair in the fetal position.

"That's what you get for ordering diner lobster every day for lunch," Kyle calls, not without sympathy.

"Let me guess. He can't go on tonight."

"The front row better have splash guards," Brick offers.

Nina holds up a hand and swivels to face the wall. I hear her counting backward from a hundred under her breath.

At ninety-six, she turns back with a sigh.

"Fuck it. We have a backup bassist. But we need another vocalist."

"What about Lita?"

The woman in question is watching me from where she's perched on the couch, a strange look on her face. "I don't know the arrangements," she says slowly.

"Then we'll have to make do without," Nina bites out.

"Haley does."

No one breathes after Lita says those words.

"Not happening."

I didn't hear Jax stalk into the room, but his response shuts me down. The finality of it is like a fist squeezing my heart.

"She's pretty good." Kyle shoves his hands in his pockets, tossing his head and making his hair fly. "I heard her in KC."

"No."

"Can I talk to you?" My gaze cuts from Jax to the bathroom.

"Talk." Jax ignores my silent request for privacy.

I focus on his stubborn gaze. "I sang four years of choir. I'm no Aretha, but I can do it. If you guys want." I acknowledge the fact that we're having this conversation in front of the entire band.

"You want fifteen minutes of fame? Is that what this is about?"

"Jesus, Jax," Lita murmurs to him.

The hand shoved through the front of his hair is impatient.

I'm hollowed out by the angst, not frustration, I recognize in his face.

My voice softens. "I don't care about being famous. I'm doing this for you. All of you," I amend, swallowing.

"Let's vote," Kyle chirps from the back of the room. "All in favor of Haley singing backup?" Kyle raises a hand.

Brick too.

Nina watches, unmoving.

Lita moves faster than I've ever seen her. "You're not even in the band," Jax snaps.

Which doesn't dissuade her.

Motion from the corner of the room draws our attention. Mace's hand is lifted half-heartedly.

Then it's gone, covering his mouth as he rolls off the chair and lurches toward the bathroom.

Jax blows out a long breath.

"Don't fuck it up, babysitter," he murmurs.

So, we're back to that, I want to say. But he's already turned and left.

I feel as if I've won, but my heart's racing so hard from what I've committed to I'm not sure anymore.

Lita approaches. "I'll help you get ready."

I go to clear it with Jerry, making sure he has what he needs for tonight. Then I meet Lita at her dressing room.

She passes me black jeans with ripped knees. I shimmy out of my own faded denim and pull them on, wincing as I work on the zipper. "I can't breathe."

"They look good. You need a top." She holds out a leather-looking halter top that has me raising my brows.

"Um, I don't have a bra for that." Plus it looks like it'd be as comfortable as wearing a plastic bag.

Duct-taped around your torso.

Under stage lights.

She stares at my chest. "You don't need one. You have a good body. Show it off a little."

Sweat breaks out on my neck. "Fine, but I'm keeping the shoes."

Ten minutes later, I'm sitting in front of the mirror while Lita rummages through a black bag too big to hold just makeup. After a brief show-down, I let her put curlers in my hair, and they tug on my scalp.

Soon my hair's been pulled out, brushed out,

pinned up at one side, and left to fall over one shoulder.

It's been a long time since I tried to look like something other than me. Serena plays dress up but, aside from lending me outfits, doesn't try to make me her Barbie. I've never really thought about how to boost my looks. Never had a reason to.

The next time I glance in the mirror, I don't recognize myself. After using an ungodly amount of willpower to resist ripping the mascara wand and pencil from her hands, my eyes are lined and sooty, my lashes long and full. Even my brows are more defined. But it's my mouth I stare at.

"It's... red."

"You hate it."

"I love it." I hold a finger over my lips, afraid to touch it.

Her hair brushes my cheek as she leans down next to me.

After Lita leaves for her set, I walk out into the hall and find Nina on the phone. She clicks off when she sees me. "Haley. Wow."

Jax emerges from the other room. "Nina, where the fuck is..."

He trails off as his gaze lands on me. I swear his jaw tightens. His eyes rake down my body, then back up. Linger on my face.

I feel hot all of a sudden despite the air-conditioned hallway.

"Haley!" Kyle calls from the open doorway down the hall, making me jump. "You're a babe."

"Thanks."

He and Brick go to pass us. Brick barely spares me a glance. Kyle grabs for my ass, and I duck out of reach in a well-practiced maneuver.

Then it's Jax and me.

It's the first time we've been alone since his dressing room. Since he sat next to me, laughed with me, told me his secrets.

Since I betrayed him.

At least, that's how he saw it.

The intensity of his expression has me looking away. My gaze lands on the table, the two passes that are still there.

My nerves and excitement wane. "Jax. Aren't Grace and Annie coming?"

That's when I notice the tension in his shoulders. "Not tonight." He clears his throat.

In a few minutes, thousands of people will be screaming his name.

At this moment, he looks completely alone.

Ignoring the buzzing in my head, I close the distance between us and throw my arms around his neck.

"Hales," he murmurs, surprised, and I feel the vibration along my skin.

I think he's going to push me away, but he doesn't.

His arms encircle my waist, and he pulls me hard against him.

Jax's breath warms my neck, and I breathe in his masculine scent.

I want to find Grace and shake her, to ask if she knows how much he worries about her. To ask if she knows how lucky she is to have someone who cares that much.

When I pull back, I swear some of the darkness is gone from his expression. "You look like you needed that."

He doesn't answer, but his gaze runs down my outfit again, ending at the floor. "Nice shoes."

I dig the toe of my Converse into the tile. "Thanks. I wanted something familiar."

Jax shifts toward the wall, tugging me with him as a tech moves past us with a piece of lighting equipment. His strong hand lingers on my arm for a beat longer than necessary, sending tingles up my spine.

"First time I played a stadium was Madison Square Garden. I'd opened for another group for a year. But when the first album caught? I'd seen hockey games from there, and all of a sudden, I was playing it."

I shake my head, feeling curls sway at my cheeks. "It must have been a trip."

His mouth twitches at the corner. "It was a total trip."

Jax may not have forgiven me, but I feel it again. That realness between us that's so precious I'm afraid to reach for it in case I tear it like tissue paper.

I hear Lita's band in the background, echoes of the second song in their set list coming down the hall. My stomach lurches.

"I know you're supposed to picture the audience naked," I whisper, "but the only thing scarier than tens of thousands of drunk people is tens of thousands of naked drunk people."

Jax inclines his head, his hair falling across his face. Maybe he forgot to gel it today, but I like it better like that.

"Do me a favor, Hales." I don't know if it's his rumbling voice or the nickname that sends my pulse skittering.

"What's that?"

"Don't ever change."

14

"Jax, it's me. I'm sorry the concert didn't happen. I had to work. I'll try again. Maybe in a week?"

I delete Grace's voicemail in the car on the way back to the hotel after the show.

Straight after the last encore, I bolted. Normally I wait for my band, sometimes even the crew.

Not tonight.

Some people don't like time alone. Me, I need to process. To turn things over, to unpack them, look at them.

But it's a fine line between that and spinning out in my own shit.

Haley knew I was pissed. What she didn't know

was that only half of it was her fault. The rest was Cross' ultimatum, fresh in my mind.

When I saw her walk into the hall wearing that outfit, her mouth painted the color of cherries...

It was all I could do not to drag her into my dressing room.

Then she'd hugged me.

I can't remember the last time a girl who wasn't my sister hugged me. I can't remember wanting one to.

I mean, it's a fucking hug. As innocent as it gets.

That's why there's no excuse for the fact that I let myself into my room, drop my shit by the door, and collapse on the bed.

The blood is pumping through my veins, and I'm alive with it.

I reach for my belt, snapping it open.

Then the button on my jeans. The zipper.

My hand is on my hard cock as I picture her singing my songs.

The way her tits looked in that top.

The curve of a smile on her red mouth when she started to relax.

I shouldn't be doing this, but I'm tired of telling myself no.

I stroke down my cock, and a long groan escapes.

Yes. This is exactly what I fucking need. My balls are tighter than Kyle's drum kit, and I know I'm going to come forever in about sixty seconds.

My hand plays my body, but it's my mind calling the shots as I imagine dragging her off stage at the end of the show. This time, instead of escaping back here, I pull her into the shadows and run my hands down her sides, over her ass. I swallow her gasp because we need to be quiet if no one's going to find us.

Because I'm sure as hell not stopping for anything short of an earthquake.

It's pain and pleasure at once, my hand moving easily thanks to the wetness already leaking from my tip. I grip my cock harder, putting pressure on the sensitive underside. Imagining it's Haley's hand and I'm telling her to be rough with me.

A knock on my door has my hand stilling.

"Jax, you in there? You seen Haley?"

It's Kyle's voice.

I've got half a mind to ignore it, but the question sinks in, along with the implication.

I shift off the bed, fastening my jeans, and cross to the door.

"She's missing?"

He holds up a glass. "I made her a drink."

The hairs rise on my neck. "Wait. Don't tell me she's partying with you."

"Yeah. She's part of the band tonight." He laughs as if he made a joke, but the idea of her drinking with the guys makes me livid.

I brush past him, going down to the room with music streaming from it and shoving inside.

She's not in there.

I try texting. Then calling.

Then without waiting for a response, I snatch up the room phone, dialing 0 and pressing the front desk clerk into giving me her room number. Then I storm down the hall and knock on the door.

No answer.

I find her at a high top table down at the bar, sitting with her computer.

She's changed. Now she's wearing shorts. The same sneakers as usual. But she still has stage hair. It's big and poufy and Country Music Award worthy.

She's also wearing something that affects me more than anything she wore on stage.

My hoodie.

I shove my hands in the pockets of my jeans.

Hard.

I shouldn't be here. Being this restless around this girl won't end well.

But I can't walk away tonight.

"Close this room," I tell the bartender. "Everyone out but her."

He nods, and I give him a moment to clear the room.

Haley doesn't notice me come up behind her. I peer over her shoulder, taking a moment to appreciate the profile of her face. Her small nose. Full lips. Dark lashes.

"Nice computer."

She smiles at my voice, before she even looks up, and my abs clench.

"How'd you find me?"

I can't help matching that smile. Raising her a smirk.

"I'm Jax Jamieson, baby." I clear my throat. "Kyle said you were unwinding with the band."

"I needed to unwind from the unwinding." She makes a face.

"What're you drinking."

"Water." Her lips twitch.

I order a bourbon from the bartender, and

Haley watches with interest as he hands it to me. "That's what Lita likes too."

"Who d'you think got her hooked on it?" I force my gaze to the screen in front of her. "This is your school project?"

Guilt washes over her expression. "Not exactly. I should be working on that, but this is something else."

I shift into the seat next to her. My arm brushes hers, but for once she doesn't jump. She doesn't even shift away.

Interesting.

Before I can make sense of that, she hits a button that makes another window pop up.

"It looks like the program Jerry uses," I observe. "But the buttons are bigger."

"I thought this might be easier for him to see. And there are prompts based on the routines we usually run. I've been interviewing him about the different venues, adding what's in his head into the code."

Her gaze turns fierce, her mouth set in a determined line.

There's no market for sound programs for users with cognitive degeneration, but it doesn't matter because Haley's worried about him.

I take a deep breath. "I know, Hales. About his Alzheimer's."

Her eyes go round, and the emotion in them turns me inside out. "Oh." Her voice is small, and un-Haley-like. "I thought I could help him."

This *girl*.

This fucking girl...

"Why do you care?"

Her mouth twitches as if she's just come up with an inside joke she's not sure about sharing with me. "You can't ask that. You care about every person on this tour. I see how you take care of them. People talk about how brilliant you are, but they don't talk about how kind. They really should."

"That's bullshit," I say softly. "I've got enough darkness in me to swallow the world, and enough scar tissue to bury it with. You? You're bright. And shiny. And so damned new it's a crime to take you out of the box."

She tucks a piece of hair behind her ear, and I have the sudden insane urge to trace the shell with my tongue.

Get a grip, I tell myself.

A smile dances on her lips. "You know the difference between you and me, Jax Jamieson?" I wait because I can't do anything else when she's looking at me like that.

"*Nothing*," she says finally. "I mean, besides the obvious."

I raise a brow. "That I'm a multi-platinum recording artist and you're a college computer whisperer."

"No!" she exclaims. "That I can't come close to peanuts and you can probably devour them by the handful."

I want to crawl inside her.

But I decided before the dangerous series of events starting in KC that she's off-limits. And in that sense, nothing's changed.

She unplugs the earbuds from her computer, wrapping the cord into a tidy little ball before her gaze comes back to mine. "I thought I'd be exhausted after tonight. It's more energy than I thought. But..."

"But you can't unwind," I finish.

Haley looks past me toward the door, the smile lingering on her lips. For the first time I notice the music in the background. Something low and bluesy.

As if deciding something, she shuts the lid of her notebook and tucks it under her arm, rising and peering down at me. "Hey, Jax," she whispers.

Electricity lights up my body. My torso tightens in anticipation. "Yeah, Hales."

"Want to get out of here?"

I know I'm going to regret this before I even shoot a look toward the door. "I have an idea."

———

The Dolly Rock-N-Bowl is open twenty-four hours, and at midnight, it's hopping.

There's no way I won't get recognized, but I grab the fake moustache I haven't used in ages and do my best incognito.

When she comes up to me, she laughs. "You look like such a redneck."

A gray-haired couple in line behind us interrupts as we're getting our shoes.

"Aren't you the cutest," the woman says. "What're your names?"

"Leonard," Haley supplies with a grin.

"And Dolly," I say, deadpan.

"Like the name of the bowling alley?"

"One and the same."

I can tell they don't know who I am, so I let down the hood of my hoodie.

"How long y'all been dating?"

We exchange a look.

"A year," I say at the same time as she says, "Two weeks."

It feels good to be anonymous, to pretend. We used to be able to get away with it, but I gave up trying two tours ago.

Tonight I need it.

We stake out our lane, and when the server comes around, I order two beers.

"Can I see your ID?" he asks Haley sheepishly.

Haley straightens and flushes. "My birthday's next week."

For a moment, I'm afraid he's going to ask for mine, but he doesn't.

I hand one of the beers to Haley when he leaves. She glances up from where she's entered Leonard and Dolly into the electronic scoring system, and I grin.

"Can I tell you something?" she says after taking a sip of her beer.

"I wish you would."

"I go back and forth between wanting to find out who my dad is and thinking I'm better off not knowing." I ignore the pang of guilt. "I finally decided to do one of those Ancestry tests. You know, the kind that checks against the general population to find people in your family tree?"

My heart thuds dully in my back. "And?"

"Nothing came back," she says. "Maybe it was an immaculate conception."

"The nuns would approve."

She laughs as she rises from the seat to throw her first ball, taking out five pins.

Guilt works through me because I'm leaving the tour, and her, and she deserves so much better than Cross.

Part of me wants to forget I ever learned they're related. She'd be better off without him.

But if he is ready to acknowledge her, apparently that comes with a trust fund. Which she could clearly use.

"My father was out of the picture by the time I started recording," I say as I watch her take out two more on her second, "but before that, he hurt my mom. Sometimes me."

Haley turns back to me, riveted. "What about your sister?"

I shake my head. "I never let him hurt Grace. I wouldn't. It was the one thing I could control. The only thing, sometimes, until I started playing guitar and singing." I go and choose the heaviest ball I can find, letting it loose. I turn back before it hits the pins at the other end. "My mom died when I was seventeen. Grace was three years younger."

It's the most I've talked about it in... probably ever, but with Haley, it comes easier than I expect.

"When I started recording those videos," I go on, selecting another ball and adjusting my angle to take out the final two pins, "it was a way to get out of my head. I never dreamed anyone would watch them. I was trying to keep food in the fridge. I tried working at a corner store. Waiting tables. Nothing stuck. When Cross showed up at my door, I thought it was too good to be true."

I cross to where she's perched on the edge of the bench, hands clasped.

"No one comes to pluck you from obscurity," I go on. "But after ten years of this, I realize how wrong I was. So much is luck and chance and the whims of men powerful enough to make you a god by snapping their fingers."

Her face is a mask of empathy. "You regret leaving."

"I should've been there to take care of them."

I offer my hand. After a moment's hesitation,

she takes it, rising, and moves past me to choose a ball.

The electricity between us is gone as quickly as it came.

She throws a decisive strike and turns on her heel. I offer her a fist bump, which she takes. "Maybe you were taking care of them here."

Her gaze is level, but I shake it off. "It's not that simple, Hales. Money doesn't fix absence."

"You hate Cross for what he did?"

"Yes," I say, though I'm sure she doesn't know what I mean. "He's used a lot of people to get where he is."

"The tour's almost over." I swear there's a note of sadness in her voice. "What're you going to do?"

"Atone." I throw again, missing entirely.

"That's not a job description."

My mouth twitches.

"Are you going to keep recording? Go on some speaking circuit?" She makes a face. "Or you could get married. Have kids."

I throw once again, this time clearing half the pins. I turn back to her as the pins reset, peering into her flushed face. "So now you're worried about me dying alone."

She skirts me, shooting a look on the way to select a ball. "Not worrying. Just wondering."

Hairs stand up on the back of my neck. "If I want company, Hales, I'll make it happen."

Something flickers through her eyes, but it's gone as fast as it came.

Haley throws, and two pins go down. I take a seat on the bench as the song in the background switches to Elvis and yellow and pink lights swirl over the lanes.

"What about you?"

"I'll go back to school, finish my program. Professor Carter is helping me. He doesn't love music like I do, but he's a coding genius." Her voice is determined as she selects her second ball.

"Professor Carter. I'm glad you've got some old guy wrapped around your finger."

"He's the same age as you."

I don't know how if she gets a strike or misses entirely because all my attention's on her. "Wait, what?"

She comes to stand in front of me, folding her arms over her chest. "Technically, he's a year younger."

She's looking at me as if I'm crazy, but I feel as though I'm the only sane person here.

I don't know if there's a right way to respond in this moment. All I know is I'm responding the wrong way.

I don't give a shit.

"Hales. You like this guy."

She flushes. I've felt a lot of dark feelings, but the one that rises up now is more jealousy than protectiveness.

And why the hell shouldn't it be? She's off-limits to me, there's no way she's going to go back to Philly and fall into the arms of some guy who should know better.

"Too bad he can't touch you."

She brushes off her hands, giving me an arch look. "Touching someone isn't always terrible. Not when it's someone I know. And when I'm in control."

"So what. You'll blow him all night but he can't go down on you?"

I shove off the bench, eliminating the inches between us. Forcing her to lift her chin and meet my eyes.

Haley's eyes widen in surprise. I know I'm out of line, but I can't seem to stop.

"Jax?" she murmurs in a voice that has me

remembering what I was doing thinking about her not even two hours ago.

"Yeah."

"You sound like you've got it bad."

Blood surges through my veins. She has no idea.

Haley points across the room. "I saw a vending machine. They probably have Snickers. You can eat it over there."

I blink.

Is she really so blind she has no idea how she affects me?

I should be grateful she's not thinking about the things we could be doing together in a hotel room right now.

"Shit, Hales. I don't need a Snickers." I let my eyes fall closed for a second, counting the breaths because I feel disoriented and it's not on account of the fake moustache.

I open my eyes, my gaze landing on her oval face, her eyes framed in extra-dark lashes leftover from the stage makeup.

"You want to know what I wrote on this sweat-shirt?" I ask. "'This is me, signing your tits'."

Haley's snort cuts the tension. "You did not."

"Did too. Says so right here." Without breaking

her gaze I trace the letters over her chest, my finger pressing into the swell of her breasts through what I'm suddenly regretting is the thickest sweatshirt in the history of the world.

Her eyes darken.

It could be innocent. It should be.

It's not.

I watch the awareness creep over her face, the realization that what I really want to do is touch her, and it's goddamned pornographic.

I'm daring her to back away.

She doesn't.

My fingers go dangerously low, and I catch the edge of one pebbled nipple.

Her eyes aren't brown or green now. They're black.

I wonder if her pulse is hammering like mine.

That's the only possible reason neither of us notices the whispers sooner.

But when I tear my gaze away from her, I can see we've been spotted. The group in the next lane has their phones out and is whispering and clicking away.

I grab Haley's arm—the arm of my sweatshirt, technically. "Time to go."

We take off across the bowling lanes before

sprinting out the door. We find a building to hide behind and collapse, breathing heavily.

She looks down and laughs. I realize we're still wearing our bowling shoes. "Is this every day for you?" she asks.

"Usually I have enough security. And I don't spend a lot of time in public like that."

I call a car to get us, and we spend a few minutes alone in the dark.

"Sorry about the quick getaway," I murmur, careful to keep my voice low.

"Are you kidding?" She pants out a laugh. "Being on that stage tonight, sharing it with you, the crowd, your music... Tonight's the best gift anyone's ever given me."

My chest tightens.

I'm a bundle of issues, and getting closer to this girl is not what I should be doing.

Haley reaches up, and I hold my breath until I feel the tugging at my lip.

She peels the moustache off, sticking it to the arm of my T-shirt like a decoration before meeting my gaze. "Better," she decides.

"I'm not a moustache guy?"

"I like you the way you are."

When the car pulls up, I follow her inside.

The Town Car's spacious enough, but it's no limo. There're a few inches of space between us. Less than the designated middle seat because one or both of us unconsciously decided that was too big a gap.

I clear my throat. "Can I ask you something?"

"Hit me." Her voice is low and soft beside me.

"What do you do when you feel trapped? I have to make a decision. Either option is bad. Both ways hurt people I care about."

I feel her gaze work over me in the dark. She doesn't press, or judge.

She wouldn't blame me for not having her back, which only makes this harder.

"You always have a choice, Jax. Kierkegaard said when you're standing on the edge of a cliff, looking down into the abyss, you're twice afraid." Her voice is low, barely audible over the running noise of the car. "Once for the knowledge that you could fall and perish. And once for the knowledge that the choice of whether to stay or whether to jump is ultimately yours.

"He called it the dizziness of freedom. Because no matter what we're given or what's taken from us... we're all free to choose how to live."

"Don't tell me this is another one of your professors."

She laughs. "Philosopher. Long dead."

"Good."

I want to shift over her, to take her mouth with mine and vanish into the blackness. To see if we can create the same bubble with our lips and tongues and hands we seem to be able to when we talk or smile or tease.

I've moved closer somehow, my arm brushing hers. Haley's shoulders tense, because we're closer than two people have a right to be. A little noise escapes from her throat, and that alone has desire pounding through my veins.

No one would know if I kissed her right now. Not Cross, not Nina, not anyone. Just her and me and the back of this Town Car.

I wait for her to push me away.

Instead, her fingers brush my cheek. It's light and innocent, but everything that isn't her fades away.

My mouth grazes her temple. The sharp intake of her breath sends the need inside me twisting tighter.

The other.

She smells like hairspray and sweat, but underneath I catch a hint of her tropical shampoo.

I already care too much, and the kicker is she's not mine to care for. Cross has more of a claim on her than I do.

Even if I wish it were otherwise...

I have nothing to give her.

Finding restraint I didn't know I had, I pull back to rest my forehead rests on hers. "Hales."

"Yeah." Her whisper is as quiet as mine in the dark.

We're sharing breath, and the twisted part is this is the closest I've felt to someone in years.

"I can't be what you want."

I expect her to protest or pull away.

Instead she smiles, the tiniest gesture in the blackness of the car, but I feel it in every part of me. "You already are."

And that, ladies and gentlemen, is the sound of a man who's well and truly fucked.

15

Tour exists in some surreal state, where the time either flies or drags.

The past four days have brought two shows. For once, it's not the shows I'm counting.

It's two sound checks, which I dodge.

It's four lunches I skip, throwing myself into writing that won't come.

It's eight interviews, each more frustrating than the last. Even though I know they serve a purpose, they feel like wasted time.

I want to shout that I'm retiring. That I'm grateful to my fans and I'd be even more grateful if they would accept my humble goodbye and promptly forget about me forever.

I owe Cross an answer tonight. There's no way he's forgotten.

If I tell him I'm out, he might take his secret to the grave. I can see him doing it just to spite me.

And even if Haley finds out—from me or someone else—he might simply deny her what she's owed. He has no obligation to provide for her, even if the thought leaves a metallic taste in my mouth.

Nothing's happened between me and Haley since Dallas. If I'm avoiding her, it's because that's the best possible way for this to play out.

When she leaves, I won't have the torture of resisting her.

I won't have any part of her.

"Jax, you have a visitor," Nina calls into my dressing room. "Technically two."

I turn to see the kid running at me. Red braids bounce at her shoulders, and her eyes are bright with eagerness. "Uncle Jax!"

My heart lifts even before I wrestle her into my arms, lifting and spinning her around. "Hey, squirt. Damn, you're getting heavy."

"You can't say that to girls," Grace chastises, right on Annie's heels.

"Which part, damn or heavy?" I shoot her a

wink, setting Annie down and wrapping my sister in a hug.

"I'm glad you made it," I murmur against her hair, a few shades darker than mine.

"We did. Finally."

I want to escape. To take off and take Grace and Annie with me.

Until last week, that was the plan.

For the first time, something's holding me back.

I don't want to leave Haley.

Not like this.

"I'm glad you came tonight."

"Me too." Grace's smile is faint in the back seat of the Town Car after the show.

Annie's curled up and half-asleep against my shoulder.

The three of us had gone to the Olive Garden and gotten a private room there. Sometimes the most comforting things aren't limos or hotel rooms —they're breadsticks.

"You're pretty good," she says.

"I've picked up a few tricks over the years." The

answer comes easily, but even I know it's not enough anymore.

I check on my niece. Annie's fast asleep between us.

"It always feels strange, seeing people cheer for you. Sometimes I want to scream at them that they don't know you at all. Like how you make the best chocolate chip cookies. How you used a nightlight until you were twelve. The way you played puppets with me when I was home alone instead of going out with your friends. That you tried to grow the world's most awful beard at sixteen and hunted down any remaining photos of it at seventeen."

I grin. "I'm glad those are the memories you have."

"I remember other things too. Us swiping food. And the games you'd play so I didn't realize we were dodging child services."

"Annie will never deal with that." It's a promise and a threat.

"Things are good. I told you."

I reach for Grace's arm and pull up the sleeve that's too long for the summer heat.

She sucks in a breath when I brush my thumb over her skin.

"Again?" I whisper hoarsely.

"Don't. Don't look at me like I'm weak. Like I'm in need of protection."

"It's getting worse."

She pulls down her sleeve. "I protected you too."

Anger burns in the back of my throat, along with regret and unfairness.

I turn her words over as the car pulls up in front of the airport, then I reach into my pocket and pull out a stack of bills. I tuck them into her hand, squeezing.

"Grace, I want you to leave. Pack a bag. Come on the tour with us. Hell, you don't need a bag, I'll buy you whatever you need. Rent you your own bus. Just don't go back there."

She blinks at me. "He's my husband. Just because things get hard doesn't mean you bail. He's been there for me."

When you haven't. Her meaning is clear.

"I'm not letting her be raised like this. I'm not letting you go through it."

"It's not your choice. Whether you come home in two weeks or two years, it still won't be."

She tries to give the money back, but I fold her hand around it. Her shoulders cave in as she pockets it. "You might get to call the shots out here, but this is my life, big brother. Our lives."

She brushes a hand over Annie's hair, and the kid stirs. I sweep Annie into a fierce hug. She laughs sleepily.

"You call me every day, yeah?" I tell Annie.

She nods.

"You happy, squirt?"

Another nod, her smile in the dark. Guilt and helplessness tear through me.

"I'll see you soon." I don't know if the words are true.

Grace shifts out of the car, tugging Annie with her. I don't want to let go. But I do.

16

HALEY

Haley,

I received your email about submitting the program to Spark. Upon review, I've decided it's not ready yet. Let's continue to work on it next semester and aim for next year's Spark competition.

I trust you'll understand.

Chris

I t's the worst sleep I've had since being on tour.

Let's be honest—I haven't been sleeping for the better part of a week.

Since on or about the night Jax Jamieson groped me in a bowling alley.

Almost kissed me in his Town Car.

Then went back to ignoring me.

Okay, ignoring isn't quite the right word.

But the morning after he'd walked me to my room and I lay in bed all night debating whether I should walk my ass down the hall and beg him to put his mouth on me?

I didn't see him until he took the stage.

The next day was almost as bad.

Yesterday, at the lunch Jax did not partake in, I overheard from Mace that Jax's sister and niece were coming. For real this time.

And I didn't get to meet them.

Maybe he decided our friendship, if you can call it that, isn't worth tolerating the monster crush I have on him, I think.

But then, he didn't seem to hate it when he was going all braille on your boobs.

It's stupid to feel hurt. I get it intellectually. Jax

is a musician, *the* musician, and I'd have to be a moron to expect anything from him.

Still, there's a tension in me I don't know how to resolve. I've tried, by throwing myself into work. Then by seeking relief late at night alone.

Any kind of relief.

This morning after getting up to Carter's delightful email, I shove my things into my bag and stab the button in the elevator.

I worked my ass off trying to finish this program, and he tossed it aside as though it didn't even matter.

Sure, I could've spent more time on it if I hadn't built the program for Jerry. Still, if Carter'd told me what more needed to be done instead of sending a dismissive email? I could've done it.

Now I'm already trying to come up with other solutions for tuition, but my mind jumps from one thing to another like cerebral Whac-A-Mole.

Part of me wants to talk to Jax. But as we pack up the bus, I realize Jax isn't the one I need to talk to.

A woman answers on the second ring. "Professor Carter's office."

I pause, tripped up by the unfamiliar voice. "Who is this?"

"Stacey. I'm Chris's research assistant. He's, ah, out this morning—" She giggles. "But he should be back this afternoon. Can I give him a message?"

"Yes. Can you tell him Haley Telfer called?"

"Haley Telfer? Sure."

"Hey, can I ask you something? How did you get this research assistant job?"

I can almost hear her shrug. "Chris just sent me an email. Around the end of the semester. You know how these things are."

"Right. Thanks."

Betrayal tastes bitter in my throat.

Carter didn't want me as his research assistant because he had another option.

Clearly he spent enough time with Stacey that he didn't have time to spend on my program.

As I walk zombie-like to the bus, Nina calls the crew together.

Still no Jax.

"I have an important announcement. As you know, we're coming up on our final shows. But I've just gotten word that because we're selling out, the tour's being extended. Two months," Nina says.

Lita's gaze meets mine, but she doesn't look surprised.

"You all have the option of staying on after the

final show or leaving," Nina continues. "But if you're leaving, I need to know now."

I don't move because every word from her mouth sounds impossible.

"Nina emailed me and my band this morning," Lita says. "It was Jax's call. And Cross's. I already told Nina we're going to Nashville tonight. She's lining up another band to open for the final two months, as well as the next two shows. You should come with us."

But I can't think about her offer because my attention's on the other bus, shining in my peripheral vision.

I go into my bag, dig out an item of clothing, and yank it over my head.

"Haley?" Lita asks. "Where are you going? We're getting ready to roll out."

"I'll be back faster than your center fielder can catch a pop fly," I mutter.

Then I stalk across the parking lot.

When I knock on the door of the other bus, Kyle's shaggy head appears. "What's up, Haley?"

Three pairs of Riot Act eyes watch me stalk toward the beaded curtain. It sings as I brush through it.

Jax looks up from his guitar. Today he's wearing a black T-shirt and jeans plus socks.

Without the stage makeup, with his hair falling over his face, he looks younger.

"Hales." His voice is wary. "You shouldn't be here."

"Yeah, well, a lot of things shouldn't happen," I inform him. "Good people shouldn't die young. Studios shouldn't reissue vinyl albums as cut from the master when they're not." I glance over my shoulder. "Kyle shouldn't answer the door wearing nothing but underwear."

He takes in my own clothing choice but doesn't comment. "The bus is leaving soon."

I ignore that. "Nina said you're extending your tour." A muscle in his jaw tics as he sets the guitar off to the side and shifts back. "So fill me in. You saw Grace and Annie last night, the people you live for, decided that was more than enough time with them and you might as well hang out on the road a little longer? That when you go back to Dallas, you'll be bored out of your skull?"

The tension in his body is a living thing as he rises from the couch and stares me down.

"I'm not explaining my choices to you. You wouldn't understand. Besides, I'll have plenty to do. I'll buy a house. The kind where the living room doesn't have wheels. And it'll have columns in the front like I'm Julius Caesar." Jax drags a finger along the door frame around the curtain, lazily following the path with his gaze. "Ten bedrooms."

His masculine scent should be a warning, but I step closer. "Why not twelve?"

He shrugs. "Sure. Fourteen."

I turn away, inspecting the photos mounted to the sides of the bus. Dozens of them. Some with the band, but more with his family.

I spin on my heel. "A pool?" I ask.

His gaze narrows. "The size of a football field."

"Do you even swim?"

"Like a fish."

The bus lurches forward, yanking me off balance. Jax grabs me by the arms to stop me from falling.

Now we're committed, because we're rolling down the road. I'm on Jax's bus and I know it's a bad idea. His expression says he does too.

"You can't be on here."

"Are you going to throw me out the window? At least let me grab a pillow off the couch. I can take the same one as last time."

His fingers dig into my skin through the fabric of the sweatshirt.

"Why are you wearing that."

"It was a gift," I remind him, my teeth grinding together as I tug on the ends of the laces through the hood. "I thought that's how gifts worked. Once they're yours, you get to use them however you want. Unless I'm wrong about that too."

When Jax's eyes darken in confusion, I know he sees the tears stinging behind my eyes. *Great*.

"What are you talking about, Hales."

This isn't why I came here. But now that Jax is holding me—okay, not quite in his arms, but between his hands—I can't lie to him.

"Carter didn't want to work with me. He wanted some girl to fawn over him." I swallow the thick feeling in my throat. "He's older and experienced and patronizing, and apparently that's my type. Which sucks because there's no way in hell a man like that would want me. For anything."

Jax stares at me like I'm speaking another language. "That's bullshit, Hales."

It's not the warning in his eyes that does me in or the way his muscles flex under the faded T-shirt. It's not the working of his jaw or the lines around his mouth or the way he stands up for me even to myself.

It's all of them.

"Jax?"

"Yeah."

"Did I do something wrong? The other night, I mean." I hate that I'm asking the question, but I need to know.

Now that we're so close, I need to know what the hell happened.

"No." He curses, his gaze working over mine. "No, you didn't do a damn thing wrong. You couldn't if you tried."

I risk a glance at his face, and his expression has me sucking in a breath.

He doesn't look angry. He looks contrite, and something I can't quite read.

"How long has it been since you touched someone?" Jax's voice is barely audible over the running noise of the bus.

"A while."

"How about since you wanted to?" God, his voice is low. If it were a color, it would be black.

I reach up to where his hair's fallen over his forehead. I tuck it back, careful not to brush his skin when I do. "Forever."

My fingers itch, and before I can stop them, my hands stretch out to graze his abs through the thin T-shirt.

The muscles there twitch under my touch, and when he drags in a rough breath, his eyes lowering to half-mast, I know what it's like to be powerful.

That's when I realize what's in his expression.

It's longing. The kind of singular wanting that comes from looking at something you can't ever have.

My touch drags up Jax's chest, exploring it the same way.

It's broad and hard, and I'm suddenly remembering how he looked when I caught a glimpse of him shirtless in his dressing room. I picture the lines and indentations as I touch him, and every brush of my hands on his body thrills me in a way I never expected.

"What's wrong?" I ask at his rough intake of breath. "You get touched by strangers every day."

My fingers continue their hypnotic path. The hem of my shirt tickles my back as I rise up on my toes so I can reach his shoulders.

"There's just one problem, Hales," he murmurs. His voice is every bit as dark as mine, as if maybe he's as lost in this spell as I am.

We're close enough his breath reaches my face when my gaze lifts to meet his. "What's that?"

His hands slide up my arms, his fingers threading in my hair and holding my head in a way that's strangely sweet and possessive at once, tipping my face up to his.

"You're not a stranger."

He smells like sandalwood and shampoo, and when my nose bumps his chin, I can't help the strangled little sound that escapes my throat.

Through my lashes, I see his mouth, firm and parted.

Full of possibility for a heartbeat. Two.

Then his lips crush down on mine.

Every cell in my body comes alive at once at the feel of his mouth rubbing, teasing, parting.

My hands band around his wrists to push him away. To get some space.

He's having none of it.

Jax isn't gentle. He's a hurricane, designed to wreak maximum devastation as he wakes up every nerve ending in my body.

He grabs my sweatshirt, raising his mouth long enough for me to gasp a breath as he yanks the fabric between us and over my head and back, trapping my arms in the sleeves behind me.

I'm struggling, but every move just brings me into closer contact with him. His mouth, his chest, his hands.

It's tearing me apart. I want to scream with it.

Instead of struggling, I go still. Force myself to focus on the gentle friction of his lips. His tongue.

In that moment, I find what I'm looking for.

Not the discordance, but the tension before the resolution.

We're a hook ready to split into a chorus.

A crowd moments from erupting...

I realize he's right.

We're not strangers.

I feel the moment my resistance dissolves, the second I kiss him back, my lips sliding under his. My tongue exploring his mouth.

Jax groans low in his throat, and it's the hottest sound I've ever heard in my life.

I struggle to get out of the sweatshirt, feeling like an Olympic champ when it falls away.

My hands find his jaw, his hair, needing to touch him. To remind myself this is real.

A bump in the road jars me, but it only makes him tighten his hold. Jax backs me against the side of the bus and slants his mouth at a new angle. His tongue finds mine, and damn if he isn't even more eloquent like this than he is with words.

He uses his hips to wedge mine against the side of the bus.

And holy damn, I'm lost.

Kierkegaard didn't know shit, because the feeling of looking over a cliff? It's got nothing on the feel of being kissed by Jax Jamieson. Being the center of his universe.

How long we kiss is anyone's guess.

In my head, it's a moment.

In my heart, it's forever.

When he pulls back, I can still taste him. My pulse hammers through my chest as my fingers brush across my lips.

Yup, still there.

Still tingling.

I bend down, retrieving the sweatshirt at my feet. There's definitely no need for it. I think I'm sweating.

But I hug it to my chest as I sneak a look up at Jax.

He stares at me, breathing hard, like he's trying to make sense of what just happened.

"I'm totally getting fired for that, aren't I?" I whisper.

His half smile pulls into a grin that melts me. "Come on. It was worth it."

A sound like rain at my back makes me jump.

"Are you kids going to fuck?" Kyle drawls. "Because if not, I need someone to battle on *Guitar Hero*."

Jax and I exchange a look. Then Jax rubs his hands over his face. "Put some damned pants on, and we'll talk."

17

HALEY

"Whoa. Twenty-one and you don't look a day over eighteen."

The familiar voice has me looking up from my spot in the booth during final sound check an hour from curtain in New Orleans. "Serena?!"

My friend drops her bag and runs at me, squealing.

I squeeze the air from her lungs. "What are you doing here?"

"Someone showed up at my door with a backstage pass and a plane ticket." She pouts. "I figured I could clear my schedule."

"Who would..." My gaze lands on the stage where Jax and his band are getting set up, and my heart expands.

Serena follows my gaze. "Damn. You have this tour thing down. Not only do you have Carter wrapped around your finger, but Jax Jamieson too?"

I shake it off. "First, there's no fingering of any kind. Second, you were right about Carter. He hired someone else."

Her jaw drops. "No fucking way."

"Yeah. He also didn't submit my program for Spark."

"Guess I'd better start dancing again to pay for rent," she jokes.

I groan.

"Fine. What about that?" Her hair flips as she jerks her head toward the stage.

I glance around before lowering my voice. "He might have kissed me on his bus yesterday."

"YES!" she squeals. "Need more condoms?"

"No. But I do have the option to stay on tour for another two months."

"In that case, you should definitely keep the condoms." Serena winks and I roll my eyes. "I knew you'd crack this whole touring thing. In fact, I figured you were on to something and thought I might apply for a part-time job in PR at Wicked during the school year."

"Really?"

"I bought internet and spent the whole flight here doing research. Looking through press files. Shannon Cross is a total hottie, by the way."

"He's too old for you."

"Watch it, pot." I shake my head. "Plus, there is no such thing. I need to show you something." She holds up her phone with a picture of a dozen or so people wearing cocktail clothes. It looks like a gala of some sort. "Anyone look familiar?"

My spine stiffens. "That's my mom."

"It says the picture is from an event a decade ago."

"Why would she be in a picture taken at a party for Wicked?"

"That's a crazy coincidence."

"Yeah. Crazy."

Something tickles the back of my mind, and I reach for my phone.

I flip through the photos. The last few weeks include ones of Kyle doing a cameo at an anti-fur rally, Mace holding up his finished Death Star, and Lita posing with a cutout of one of her fantasy baseball pitchers whom she's sworn she'll marry once she retires.

I scroll back to the picture I took of the photo

in Jerry's album. The woman who bore a vague resemblance to a woman I knew more than anyone.

I'd been meaning to look into it, but it had fallen down my list of priorities.

"Shit. Did she ever mention him?"

"No." My heart stops. "Can you just... stay a minute. I'll be right back."

I grab her phone and make my way up the aisle toward the stage and find Jax in the wings, bent over his guitar. "Hey."

"Hi." He looks around, then back at me. His eyes darken, and I wonder if he's remembering yesterday's kiss too.

But we're not alone here, and now's not the time.

"Thank you," I say at last. "For the birthday present."

Jax's mouth twitches. "You're welcome. I tried to have her wrapped, but apparently it's a liability issue." I can't quite find it in me to laugh, and he picks up on that immediately. "What's wrong."

"Listen, I need to ask you something. I know you hate Cross, but you also know him better than anyone." I take a deep breath. "Do you know the woman in this picture?"

I show him the one from ten years ago, study his face as he scans the image.

"It would've been around the time you started at Wicked."

He shakes his head, slow.

"It's my mom, Jax. Apparently Cross knew her, or she knew Wicked. As far as I know, she never worked there, and I would've been ten when this was taken. But I can't help wondering if he might know who my father is."

Jax is watching me. I've never seen him so still.

As if in slow motion, he takes off his guitar, folding the neck strap as he lays it on the table next to him.

"Jax." My voice sounds tinny in my ears. "What aren't you telling me?"

He rubs a hand over his neck. "I don't know what to say."

"Try."

"Haley... he knows who your father is. He knows because he *is* your father."

The noise around me fades to nothing.

My brows pull together because nothing's making sense right now. "What? For a second I thought you said Cross is my father." I laugh, but he doesn't follow my lead.

"Oh wow. You actually think he is. Why..." I shove a hand through my hair. "Why would you think that?"

"Because he told me."

I picture the cool, calculating man in the suit who'd watched me the day I went into his office. There's no way we have a connection. Especially not one like that.

But the expression on Jax's face tells me it's true.

Jax reaches out, but I back away.

"You *knew*," I whisper. "And you didn't tell me."

Someone hollers his name from across the stage, and he curses. "We'll talk about this later."

I turn on my heel and start back to the sound booth. The seats blur into smudges as I stalk down the row.

My mind runs on logic, but it's like some tiny, desperate part of me has taken the wheel and I've jumped the tracks.

Shit, even my metaphors are chaos right now.

I can't help it. Over and over, it runs through my head.

Jax knew.

Why didn't he tell me?

And then,

Is that why I'm here?

That's why I was chosen over two hundred applicants.

Cross picked me.

When did Jax know?

Did he know when he sat across from me in that car and threw his Snickers bar out the window?

When he took me bowling and we talked in the back of the car?

He sure as hell knew when he kissed me.

The knot in my stomach grows into a darkness that seeps into every muscle. Every pore.

"Your friend Jerry said the ticket holders are getting let in soon." Through my blurry vision, Serena's face comes into focus. "Haley, what's wrong?"

It takes everything in me to keep my voice level. "I'm wrong. I was wrong about everything."

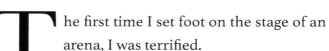

18

The first time I set foot on the stage of an arena, I was terrified.

But the same thing that scared the shit out of me then became the thing that made me invincible.

The audience. Every pair of eyes trained on you, every person invested in what you're about to do for them, create with them, makes you stronger.

Being onstage in front of twenty thousand people is like being immortal.

I don't care what you're guilty of. All of it melts away for a few hours here, under the lights.

Each night I'm Icarus, flying into the sun.

Too high to see that every move I make brings me closer to my own destruction.

At least that's how it's always been.

Tonight, I feel her eyes on me from the booth.

Though I can't see her, as the curtain rises and we break into our opening number, I pretend I can.

She's judging me.

She deserves to.

We blaze through the set list. Each song gets all of me because holding something back would be a bigger crime.

At the end, I turn to Mace and mutter in his ear.

His eyes widen. "Seriously?"

He goes to Kyle, who locks eyes with me, but I'm already turning back to my mic stand.

You're standing on the edge of a cliff, looking down into the abyss, and you're twice afraid.

Once for the knowledge that you could fall.

And once for the knowledge that the choice of whether to stay or whether to jump is yours.

The arena's silent as I wrap my hands around the mic, and for the first time in a long time, I'm exposed.

"There are moments that define us, for better and for worse. This song reminds me of the darkest time in my life. A time I wanted to leave behind. But the reason I'm playing it is a bright one." I swallow. "A hopeful one."

Cries start up, but I ignore them as I do something I haven't done in ten years.

I play "Inside."

And it's not for my band, or the fans.

It's for *her*.

I told Cross I would do the extra two months of shows because I've been dealing with the fallout from Grace and Annie for years. I may not be able to make up for that, but for the first time, I have hope that I can.

Especially if she's here.

The crowd deafens me as we finish the number and leave the stage.

Mace calls after me, but I ignore him, winding through the backstage corridors to my dressing room.

There's a girl in there, and for a split second, I imagine she's Haley.

She can't be. She's taller with blond hair. Plus she's dressed up.

"Jax."

"Who are—"

"Serena. Haley's friend."

I notice the backstage pass swinging around her neck. "Right. Where's Haley?"

"She left."

My eyes fall closed. "Left for where?"

When she doesn't answer, I glare at her.

"You can't scare me with that look. I'm going to tell you because I think you guys should talk but not because you look like you'll kill me if I don't." She takes a breath. "She's going to Nashville. Tonight."

I spin on my heel and stalk down the hall.

19

HALEY

Two months later

"There you go, darlin'."

My fingers grab the fifty the second it hits the sticky counter. The money is soft, frayed, as if it's done this a million times before. "Thanks. I'll be right back."

"No change." The guy flashes me a grin, and I make change in the register before putting the rest in the tip jar. "Since it's windin' down in here, why don't we have a drink?"

I round the bar to put the stools on tables and collect the salt and pepper shakers, flashing the automatic smile I've learned in the last two months. "I'm a little out of my league drinking that bourbon."

He follows, and the hairs on the back of my neck stand up. His gaze crawls up my legs under the short denim skirt that's practically a uniform here in Nashville.

I pray he's not going to do something stupid.

My manager's in the back office, talking to our bouncer.

Or possibly doing something else, which I definitely don't begrudge them doing because they got married last year and have had zero time together.

I should've closed up twenty minutes ago but got lost doing dishes.

"Sweetheart, I been in here three times this week. Ain't never seen you with a man."

I sense it before I feel him graze my back. Before I smell the booze on him. "Then your vision's 20/20."

"Maybe you like to play hard to get." He leers and reaches for me.

But before his hand grabs my ass through my jean skirt, the industrial salt shaker in my hand catches him in the junk hard enough his eyes bulge.

The beauty of the salt shaker. Small enough to

be used as a defensive weapon. Sturdy enough not to break when you can a guy with it.

He writhes on the floor, adopting the fetal position like it's his job.

"Hey!" Andre's baritone hollers from the back doorway.

The guy pulls himself up and slinks out the door. I lock it behind him.

"You okay Haley?" Andre's thick brows draw together on his forehead. He's lost his cowboy hat somewhere in the thirty minutes since I saw him last, and his hair's a mess.

"Peachy." I say it with more confidence than I feel.

He studies me, hard, but decides not to press it. "I'll clean up in the back if you finish up here. And don't forget this." He fishes in the cash register where an envelope's wedged in the side and hands it to me. "Your bonus."

"Thanks."

He retreats with a salute and Lita sidles up. "Last night in Nashville."

"You guys were great," I say as I grab the last of the salt shakers and bring them behind the bar to refill. "Sorry the Dodgers lost."

"S'okay. Kershaw's killing it on the season.

Which means I still have the best pitching rotation in the league."

Lita looks pointedly at my bare legs, wiggling her eyebrows. "I see you working it over there."

"Two months in this place has given me a whole new outlook on life." I lift the hem of my shirt, sniffing. "Plus clothes that'll never stop smelling like rye."

I pop open my laptop behind the bar. "I chose my classes for the fall semester. Midnight tonight"—it's after two now—"we're supposed to get our final schedule."

"You have enough for tuition?"

"Yup. Thanks to my miniskirt." She laughs.

I scroll down the page, scanning for the confirmation.

"What the..." I start. Lita peers over my shoulder. "It says I'm not enrolled."

There must be a mistake. I submitted the report on my co-op term on schedule. Early, actually.

I click through the webpage to the co-op section. There're a bunch of green checks, and at the bottom...and a red X where it says "employer verification."

"What's happening?" Lita asks.

"I have no idea."

I pull out my phone and dig up a number I've never had to use. It rings twice.

"Hi, Nina."

"Haley?"

"Sorry to call so late."

"The best time for everything is the present. In fact, it's the only time there is." Muffled scratching comes over the line.

"My letter—the one confirming my co-op term was completed—it looks like the college didn't receive it."

I hold my breath, praying she'll say something like, "Namaste, it'll be fixed by morning."

What she says instead shatters all my hopes.

"Cross hired you. It's him you need to call."

A stone settles in my stomach.

Cross is the last person I want to talk to.

Because a major record exec is my father and I haven't decided what the hell do to about it.

"Right," I murmur, realizing she's still waiting for a response. "How's the tour?"

"Insane. Riot Act announced this is their final month of concert dates. All the crazies are coming out." I heard about that announcement. Because I have a news alert on the tour. Stalkerish? Maybe.

I shove my hands in my pockets. "Nina... is the everything okay?"

A pause. "We beefed up security. Jax still has all his body parts, far as I know. We're in Atlanta tomorrow if you want to see for yourself."

"Haley, I have to run. We're getting some spec changes for the show tomorrow. Then I need to get in some meditation time so I don't accidentally kill someone. Namaste."

"Namaste," I echo as Nina hangs up. I meet Lita's clear blue gaze over the tip jar she's splitting into piles for the servers who worked tonight.

"You're thinking about something, and it's not calling Cross," Lita guesses.

Sleeping on someone's couch for two months has a way of breaking down walls between you. But I haven't been able to bring myself to tell Lita that Jax knew about Cross.

That being around Jax stirred up all these feelings I never thought I'd feel for anything that wasn't music.

That leaving hasn't brought the relief I'd hoped for. Instead, I've lain awake more nights than not, wondering if I did the right thing.

"It's nothing. It's just...Jax and I used to talk. I know this sounds insane, but I feel like I got him."

"Normally, I'd say that's completely insane," she agrees. "But Jax doesn't make time for just anyone." I turn that over in my mind as she hands me the stack of bills that's my share. "But? What does it matter. You're going to go back to Philly, and classes, and listening to vinyl or whatever you do at home."

Lita's words echo dully in my chest.

My fingers inch toward the keys of my laptop. Before I can stop myself, I'm pulling up a ticket resale site.

"Damn." Even the nosebleeds are more than my monthly groceries.

Lita drums her fingers on the bar, her mouth pursed. "I bet he'd get you a pass in a heartbeat."

"That would mean telling him."

I reach into my pocket and open the envelope from Andre. A thick stack of twenties peers up at me.

"If you're not going to talk to Jax, why go at all?"

I suck in a breath as my finger hovers over the buy button. "Closure."

Thank you for reading Good Girl! I hope you loved Jax and Haley.

Want more rock stars, brainy girls, best friends, and band mates? Find out whether Jax and Haley find their way back to each other when the tour wraps and the lights go down in **Bad Girl...**

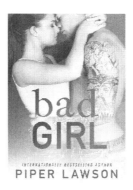

Rockstars don't chase college students.
But Jax Jamieson's never followed the rules.
I wonder why he's here.
I wonder what took him so long.
I wonder what he's going to do to me when I get off this stage...

One-click Bad Girl Now!

If you want even more, subscribe to my Insiders List. You'll hear about new books, sales, and special deals: **http://eepurl.com/bNQmYT**

I appreciate your help in spreading the word, including telling a friend. Reviews help readers find books! Please leave a review on your favorite book site.

Enjoy this book?

Here's how you can help (in two minutes or less)

I'm going to share something kind of personal. Something I haven't shared with that many people in my life...

I want to write full-time. There it is.

It always seemed crazy, but guess what. After three years of writing on midnight caffeine trips after long days at the office, I'm so close I can taste it.

You can help me make the final push. (Yes, YOU!)

I don't have the advertising budget of a big publisher. But I do have something that's worth way more.

The most amazing readers in the world.

Honest reviews are the best way to get the word out about my books. If you loved this (or one of my other books!), I'd be beyond grateful if you could take two minutes to leave a quick review.

Thanks for being awesome, for inspiring me every day, and for helping make it possible for me to do something I love.

xx

Piper

ALSO BY PIPER LAWSON

TRAVESTY

Schooled

Stripped

Sealed

Styled

Satisfaction

PLAY

PLAY

NSFW

RISE

WICKED

Good Girl

Bad Girl

Wicked Girl

ABOUT THE AUTHOR

I read and write stories where the girls aren't doormats, the guys aren't asshats, and secondary characters aren't second-class citizens. A card-carrying millennial, I have two business degrees and zero hope of starting a fashion label (unlike my Travesty characters). I crave quirk the way some people crave kink, and believe life is too short not to do what—and who—you love.

My home base near Toronto, Canada is shared with my wonderful sig other. I know he's the perfect man because not only is he TDH (tall dark & handsome), but he will beta read for me under duress. And really, that's what love is. Beta reading under duress.

To my readers: I'm beyond grateful to you guys who make it possible for me to write. Thank you for buying my books. And inspiring me. And sending me wacky ideas. You're the reason I keep doing this.

I love hearing from you! Stalk me on:

The Interwebs➜www.piperlawsonbooks.com

Facebook➜www.facebook.com/piperlawsonbooks

Twitter➜www.twitter.com/piperjlawson

Goodreads➜www.goodreads.com/author/show/13680088

THANK YOUS

This book wouldn't have happened without the support of my awesome advance team and reader group (ladies - thank you for the support, nail biting, and patiently rocking in the corner while I finished part 3). Pam and Renate, thank you for your eagle eyes! Nothing gets by you. Mandee, thank you for creating Jax's rock star-worthy signature, Jax is at least 20% more badass now. Natasha, you are the most amazing designer, thank you for letting me tweak this until we got it just right. Lindee, I couldn't imagine better photography to inspire my books. Cassie and Devon, thank you for questioning, polishing, and pointing out I meant to say IV chord, not iV chord. Danielle, thank you for the amazing promo graphics, and generally helping me stay organized and making sure I don't release new books in a vacuum. Plus of course Mr. L, the world's best beta reader and the guy who makes sure my world doesn't break while I'm sequestered in my writing cave. Thank you all from the bottom of my heart.

Printed in Poland
by Amazon Fulfillment
Poland Sp. z o.o., Wrocław

57439543R00139